Everly

Striking Back: Book One

S.M. SHADE

Cover Art by Kellie Dennis at Book Cover by Design:
www.bookcoverbydesign.co.uk

Interior Formatting by That Formatting Lady:
www.facebook.com/ThatFormattingLady/

Chapter One

Horns honking, angry voices cursing the rush hour traffic, the smell of exhaust, yeah, I'm home. "Welcome back, chick," Amy exclaims with a grin, sliding into the booth at Huddleston's, our favorite diner. "How was your trip?"

"I'm covered in mosquito bites, sunburned, and I think I have poison ivy. It was amazing."

Amy's face scrunches. "Sounds awful."

"The air in Tennessee is so clean. You can actually breathe without tasting the air. I swear I never realize how much the city stinks until I leave for a few days. The kids had a blast. We spent the days at the lake and had a campfire every evening. We slept in tents and roasted hot dogs for breakfast."

"Everly, every now and then I'm tempted to check your panties for a set of balls. You're such a guy."

"Keep your hands out of my panties," I reply, tossing a straw wrapper at her. Amy is one of my oldest friends and one of only two people in the world I actually trust.

"Speaking of balls, tell me you got some action from that blond cutie that was chaperoning with you."

"The momma's boy?" I scoff. "Hardly. He wouldn't even join in the mud fight with the kids. A grown man that's afraid to get dirty? I'll pass."

"That's your requirement of your dates? They have to like dirt?"

"They have to be a man. Real men get dirty."

"I know you like them dirty."

Lacy, our waitress, arrives with our usual order of waffles and orange juice. "Eat up girls. You're too skinny."

"And you're far sighted." I laugh. "You hire a new girl?"

Lacy glances at the harried looking girl taking orders across the aisle. "We'll see how long this one lasts. If she makes it through race weekend, I'll make her a name tag." Amy steals a slice of strawberry from my plate as a group of three men come in and sit a few tables away. "Whew, girls, must be my lucky day," Lacy mumbles, darting away to wait on them. I don't blame her. All three are cover model material, muscular, tan, and sweaty from the early spring heat wave.

Amy fans herself. "God, he's almost hot enough to make me reconsider my no dick policy. Did you see those eyes?"

I can hardly miss them since they're locked on mine. Bright, cornflower blue and so intense. A smug little smile lifts his lips and he winks at me. Great. Into the arrogant asshole file he goes. "He's not bad," I remark.

I try to focus on my food and our conversation, but he's distracting. As if the eyes and fantastic body aren't enough, tattoos sleeve one arm and disappear under his shirt only to peek out his collar. His ink black hair hangs messy and wild around a face that would stop any woman in her tracks. This guy has trouble scrawled all over him.

"Ev…" Amy snaps her fingers, laughing. "Everly! Get a grip. You look like you're going to throw him down on the table and ride him like a circus pony."

"Sorry, I was…daydreaming."

"You mean dayfucking. Go talk to him."

A quick bite of my waffle gives me a chance to consider my response. "No way. That guy has danger stamped all over him. I don't do bad boys."

"You don't do anybody."

"How are things with Wendy?" I ask, desperate to change the subject.

"Subtle, chick. We hung out again all weekend and I met

her friends. She wants me to meet her family." She looks up with a grimace.

"Are you ready for that?"

"I don't know, but, I think we'll be together awhile so..." She shrugs.

"Holy shit. Is Amy Blaine entering a serious relationship?" Smiling, I peek out the window. "It doesn't appear that hell has become a glacier, but..."

"Shut up! I didn't say that."

"Are you in love with her?" Amy remains silent, but a slow smile spreads across her face as she lays a twenty dollar bill on the table next to the check. Before she can escape, I grab her in a quick hug. "I'm happy for you, girl."

"Thanks. I have to run. I'm late for work. Tell Ian I said hi."

"I'll call you later," I reply, following her toward the door and trying to ignore the tatted Adonis as he meets my gaze again.

"Have a good day, ladies," he says, his voice smooth and deep.

"Thanks. You, too."

Amy laughs at my flippant reply. We step out into the heat. "Do you need a cab?"

"No, I'm going to grab a few things from the drugstore and stop in the bank."

"Okay, see ya." Amy's long blond waves bounce on her shoulders as she signals for a cab. Two taxis pull up instantly and I shake my head in amusement. Amy is my age, but aesthetically we're complete opposites. She's that perfect five pound blond all women love to hate. Beautiful face, beautiful body, and a great personality to boot. It's enough to make you sick. My common brown hair, brown eyes, and fat ass make me invisible to the opposite sex when I'm with her. Still, it's amusing to watch men trip over their tongues when she enters the room, knowing they aren't even on her radar.

Amy's in love. Who would've thought? We met in our last year of high school seven years ago and we've been through a lot together. She was by my side through my horrible breakup with Sean, and I helped her through her struggle to come out to her family. She's the closest thing to family I've ever known.

After half an hour in line at the drugstore, my patience is thin. All I needed was a stick of deodorant and nail clippers for hell's sake. Sweat drips down my sides as I enter the bank, the push of cold air like heaven on my clammy skin. At least the line isn't too long.

My breath catches in my throat when I look up from my phone into an intense blue gaze. He's here. The hunk of inked up sex from the diner stands at the last teller window, a small smile on his face. His eyes travel from my feet to my head, dissolving every stitch of clothing in the process. Shit, Everly, don't look at him. I'm not unattractive in a "she never outgrew her tomboy phase" sort of way, but this guy is miles out of my league.

A sudden pop behind me causes my ears to ring and cold fear trickles down my spine. When I turn to face the source of the gunshot, I'm horrified to see four men with automatic weapons blocking the exit, their faces hidden behind white Playboy Bunny masks. Fuck me. It's The Naked Bandits.

A viral sensation the cops can't seem to catch, they strike small banks in the mid-morning lull. They're typical armed robbing assholes except for one thing. They force the employees and bystanders to strip. Cops can't say if it's a strategy to keep people from running, a way to fuck with people's heads and keep them under control, or if they're just perverts who get off on watching naked people. On the plus side, they never hurt anyone, and even remove the children and elderly to an office before the skin fest begins.

The largest of the four bandits leaps to the counter, his voice carrying across the room. "You lucky fucks are in the presence of greatness. I'm sure you've heard of us so you know the routine. Get it all off and nobody gets hurt. Don't be shy, now. You, sweetheart." He gestures to the teller. "Fill up those bags. Don't even think about hitting an alarm or you'll be responsible for the pile of naked bloody bodies I'll leave behind." Nodding, the poor woman goes from drawer to drawer, filling the bag.

His skinny partner stalks through the center of the room, sweeping the assault rifle over our heads. "He said get naked, bitches! What are you waiting for?"

Shit. This can't be happening to me. Especially not in front of the tatted Adonis. My hands tremble as I pull my shirt over my head, revealing my plain cream colored bra. Is it weird that I'm more embarrassed than afraid? I'm not skinny by any account, but I'm not ashamed of my size eight curvy shape. Usually. Of course, I'm not typically naked in a room full of men, one too gorgeous to be real.

Glancing around me, I see the others slowly removing clothing. A couple in their fifties huddle together, the man shielding his wife's nudity as best he can. Two burly men who look like construction workers stand side by side, hands over their privates. A sympathetic pang shoots through me at the sight of two obese ladies, formerly dressed in designer clothes, lowering their panties with tears running down their faces. What a nightmare.

My face ignites as I slip off my shorts, exposing my blue cotton boyshort panties that just scream sexy. Apparently, I'm not moving fast enough for the third gunman and he steps in front of me with a sneer. "All of it, sugar."

"Don't touch her." A cold voice cuts through the room, silencing the sobs and whimpers. I know that voice. When I dare to look up, I'm met by those intense cornflower blue eyes. Completely naked, Mr. Adonis steps between me and the asshole with the gun.

"You want to be a hero? I can get your face all over the news. Give you fifteen minutes of fame when you're the first to die."

"Stop!" I cry. "I'm doing it! Don't hurt anyone, please." I unfasten my bra and rip down my panties before I can chicken out. At least I waxed. The stupidity of that thought makes me giggle. The gunman moves away, but my protector stays in front of me, shielding me from the view of the others.

His eyes never drop below my chin when he faces me. "Are you okay?"

"Yes," I whisper, one arm draped across my breasts, my hand cupped between my legs. "Just wondering if one can die from embarrassment."

"No one can see you right now."

"You can."

"I'm trying not to look." My face grows warmer at the sight of his impish grin.

"I appreciate that. I promise to keep my eyes above your waist." There's plenty to look at there. A chiseled chest and rippling abs lead down to a trim waist and hips, the distinctive v of abdominal muscle stretching down to...

"Ahem," He clears his throat. Shit, that's not keeping it above the waist. "After the way you were checking me out in line, feel free to have a peek, love." His voice is thick with amusement.

"The grandma and the designer sisters are gawking at your ass. Isn't that enough attention?"

"I don't want their attention." Is this seriously happening right now? Am I dreaming? Did someone slip acid in my orange juice? I'm standing in the middle of a bank robbery, bare ass to the wind while a nude muscled god flirts with me. Two of the bandits lead the bank manager back to open the safe while the other two guard a group of naked hostages intent on staring at the floor.

"Do you always hit on naked women in banks?"

"Only the beautiful ones."

"I guess you really didn't peek."

A chuckle rattles his chest. "I promise I didn't see anything...below the waist." Way to say you saw my tits, asshole. "What?" he says, a little grin lifting his lips at my glare. "Above the waist was the deal, wasn't it?" We're interrupted by the bandits ordering everyone to lie face down on the floor.

"Guess that's about to change," I groan, lying on my belly. No way to hide my ass in this position. My eyes betray me by sneaking a peek at his round cheeks.

"I'm Mason, by the way." Propping his chin on his elbow as if he's just lounging in his living room, he waits for me to reciprocate.

"Mason, thank you for protecting me. I'll admit our little conversation made this situation far more bearable, and the sight of your toned ass didn't hurt. I've had quite enough humiliation for one day so please don't be offended when I say I hope we never see one another again."

"You get to check out my ass and I don't even get your name?"

"It's Everly," I reply with a sigh.

"Well, it's been fun, Evie. And we'll see each other again." Before I can respond, the S.W.A.T. team storms into the building, long minutes after the bandits have fled.

My next two hours are spent being questioned by FBI agents. The burglars wore masks and saw us naked. How many ways do they want to hear me say it? Their questions are exhausting and when I'm finally free to go all I want is a nap. At least I manage to leave while they're still questioning Mason in another room. This whole thing was humiliating, the only saving grace that I'll never have to see any of these people again.

The city bustles and blares around me on my walk home, but I'm lost inside my own head. It's a wonder I don't get run down in the street. Indianapolis isn't known for its patience.

"Good afternoon, Ms. Hall." Jeremy, the doorman greets me as I zombie my way through the lobby of my building.

"Afternoon," I mumble, rushing into the elevator and up to my fifteenth floor apartment. Locking the door behind me, I shed my clothes on my way to bed and curl up under the comforter, blocking out this shitty morning. It's after five when my phone wakes me. A familiar face grins at me from the screen. "Hey, Ian."

"Hey, Ev. We still meeting at Mann's Grill?"

"Yep. I need a roast beef manhattan in the worst way."

"Bad day?"

"Oh, you know, met Amy for breakfast, shopped a little, had to strip naked in front of a bunch of strangers at gunpoint, the usual."

"Holy fuck, Everly! You were at Mideastern when it got hit? Are you okay?"

"I'm fine."

"They said there were shots fired."

"One shot. Into the ceiling."

A relieved sigh rattles the speaker. "Ev, are you sure you're okay? I can just come over there and bring takeout from Mann's."

"I'm fine, but I'm not going to argue with a meal on wheels tonight. Supernatural is on at eight."

"I'll be there in an hour, pup."

Amy may be my go-to for guy advice and other general girl stuff, but Ian is my rock. We were placed in the same group home when I was ten. I was pissed off and miserable, refusing to talk to anyone or participate in anything. It didn't endear me to the other kids. When two boys cornered me, threatening to jump me unless I showed them my non-existent tits, Ian came to my rescue. He got a bloody nose for his trouble, but they never bothered me again. I stuck close to him after that, or in his words, I "followed him around like a lost pup".

We kept in touch when he aged out of the system. He went to college on the state's dime and moved on to become a very successful accountant. I'm still amazed at the man that gruff, sullen teenager grew to be.

An hour after our call, Ian stares at me over my dining room table, jaw agape as I recount my eventful morning. "He stepped between you and the gunman, then blocked you from being seen by the others? Did you get this white knight's phone number?"

"Of course not!" My wadded up napkin bounces off his forehead.

"Why the hell not?"

"You didn't see the guy. Way out of my league. Plus, he saw me standing naked in public. It was humiliating."

Ian's dark brown eyes meet mine and he frowns. "No one is out of your league. How many times do I have to tell you that? He obviously liked what he saw. And you need to get back out there. Don't let one disastrous relationship ruin your chance to find a decent guy."

"My head is filled with clichés of glass houses, pots, and kettles."

"I date!"

"You don't date. You fuck. A different girl every week, seems like."

"So I like to shop around before I settle."

"Well, you're going to run out of floor models to sample if you aren't careful. You need a good woman."

He tugs me onto the couch and slings his arm around my neck. "I have a good woman."

"One who also sleeps with you." A teasing smile curves his lips, and I smack his arm. "Quit it. We tried that, remember?"

His wind mussed hair flops over his forehead as he shakes his head, laughing. "I'll never understand how two gorgeous people can love one another yet have zero chemistry."

"Can I borrow some of your arrogance?"

"Confidence. And yes, if you use it to get laid."

"Shut up. Sam and Dean are on," I exclaim, turning up the T.V. and leaning my head on his shoulder as Carry on my Wayward Son begins to play.

"Dean is such a badass."

"You have a man crush on him."

"Go fuck yourself, Ev."

"You'd totally blow him if you had the chance." A yelp escapes my throat when he pinches the back of my arm. His fingers thread through my hair, a comforting gesture we always share. "Thanks for coming. I needed this."

"I got you, pup."

Chapter Two

Determined to get back to normal, I ring the back buzzer at Striking Back at ten the next morning. "ID, honey." Aggie's voice says through the speaker as I hold my driver's license up to the camera. Of course she recognizes me, but this place houses abused women and children. They can't be too careful.

"Five-by," I reply cheerfully. Jensen, the guy who manages security for Striking Back is an ex-military man. Apparently, five-by-five was military code for "all clear", but we use our version to mean "everything's fine". In this case, I'm not being threatened by some crazy jilted husband into letting him through security. I'm buzzed inside where I nearly get bowled over by Ms. Den.

"Thank god! We've got a large donation in Bloomington and need someone to make the trip out there." Ms. Den is the head counselor at S.B. but everyone calls her the house mother. Plump and friendly, she's the backbone of this place and everyone loves her.

"Bloomington? That's an hour away." An hour sitting in traffic on the highway, ugh.

"I know, dear, but they're donating beds, mattresses, and clothing. We can't pass it up. You can take the van. They'll load it for you."

"Alright, give me ten minutes to say hi to the kids and grab a drink."

"Sure thing. I'll have someone bring the van around."

"Ev-ly!" I'm tackled by forty pounds of overexcited four year old girl.

"Hey, munchkin! What are you doing today?"

"Mommy got a job so I'm playing with Ms. Bini. I'm posed to be good."

"That's great! Are you coloring a picture?"

"Yep, a flower, wanna see?" Her sticky hand grabs mine, pulling me to the children's table where Sarah smiles at me, surrounded by three preschool age kids.

"Good morning," she says with a laugh.

"Good morning. Lana found a job?"

"Yes, ma'am, a good one too. Glenn, Bloom, and Chester law firm hired her as an assistant. If it works out, they'll pay for her to take classes to become a paralegal."

"That's fantastic." It looks like Lana and her daughter, Jamie, will be a success story. Sometimes, they're hard to come by. So many domestic violence survivors return to their abusers. Lana and Jamie came to us nearly a month ago, both covered in bruises, with nothing but the clothes on their backs.

S.B. housed them, provided lawyers to expedite her divorce, and helped with restraining orders. Thankfully, Jamie isn't the husband's child, so he has no visitation rights. Now Lana is on her way to a successful career. My heart feels lighter. I needed some good news today.

"Is Molly here?" Taking another volunteer along for the ride would at least alleviate the boredom of sitting in traffic.

"No, only the tutors and staff are here today."

"Okay, well, I have to run. Mattresses to haul, you know."

"You're a dear," Sarah says with a laugh.

As I make my way through the kitchen, Ms. Den calls to me. "Everly, hang on, I found someone to go with you."

"Great, they can drive."

Ms. Den laughs. "He's waiting in the van."

"Clear the door!" I call to Aggie, slipping my purse over my shoulder as I approach the back exit.

She checks the cameras to be sure no one is lurking to force their way inside and replies, "Door's clear! Drive safe, honey."

My phone chirps with a text from a member of my book group, reminding me of tonight's meeting. I'm texting a reply as I hop into the passenger seat of the van.

"Buckle up, Ms. Hall." His smooth voice fills my ears, and my stomach plummets to my toes. It's the tatted Adonis. I'm halfway out the van door when strong fingers wrap around my wrist. "Hey, Evie, relax. I didn't mean to scare you. I'm driving us to Bloomington."

"Let go of me! What are you, some kind of stalker?"

"Evie, if you give me a second to explain…"

"Then explain. How the fuck do you know my last name, or that I volunteer for Striking Back? How did you find me?"

"Everly, I'm the founder of Striking Back. It's my organization."

"Bullshit! S.B. was founded by Mason…" My eyes fly up to meet his, and he releases my arm. "Shit. You're Mason Reed."

"It's nice to meet you, Ms. Hall, although I have to say, you curse an awful lot. To answer your second question, I run a background check on all volunteers that work with S.B. and that typically includes your last name." A small grin settles on his face as he waits for me to connect the dots.

"You recognized me at the diner?"

He nods.

Oh no. "And at the bank." My head falls into my hands.

"Yes," he admits.

"The day that just won't die. I wasn't supposed to see you again after…all that."

"To be fair, you saw much more of me." His eyes twinkle and his wicked grin makes me laugh, though I try not to. "Close the door, Evie. We have furniture to pick up."

"The founder and CEO runs errands?"

"When it buys me time with a beautiful young girl."

"Laying it on a bit thick, aren't you?" I snort, giving in and shutting the door.

"Nothing but the truth, love."

"You're the first non-English person I've ever heard use

love as an endearment."

"I spent a few years in London and some of the local dialect seeps in." My eyes are drawn to the flex of his arms while he steers the van onto the highway. Would it kill him to wear a shirt that isn't a size too small? His biceps are trying to bust through the cotton. "Put your seatbelt on."

"Excuse me?"

"Put your belt on, Evie. We're getting on the highway." I usually do wear a seatbelt, but his demand sort of pisses me off. "What?" he asks, as I stare at him.

"I'm trying to find a less juvenile way to say 'don't tell me what to do.'"

He rolls his eyes. "Ms. Hall, will you please buckle up and set my mind at ease?"

Fastening the belt, I mumble, "It's not like I'd stick you with the ticket."

"I'm more concerned with keeping you on the right side of the windshield."

I don't have a response for that. After a few minutes, I blurt, "You don't look like the CEO of an organization."

I'm rewarded with his sexy laugh. "Oh? What does a CEO look like?"

"I don't know. Old, fitted suits, less tats."

"I own a few suits. Tell me about yourself, Evie. We have an hour drive ahead of us."

"Well, for starters, my name is Everly. My friends call me Ev."

With a little side glance, he asks, "Are you single, Evie?" I don't know whether to choke him or jump in his lap.

I take a sudden interest in the scenery flowing past my window. "Yes, with every intention of staying that way."

"That's good."

"It is?"

"Yes, that attitude will keep other men away while I wear you down."

"I'm not very susceptible to badgering."

"I can be very persuasive. I'll make a pest of myself."

Laughing, I turn the radio to a classic rock station. "Some willing woman will fall at your feet and I'll be off the hook."

He turns and flashes a crooked smile. "I don't give up, love. In fact, I'll bet you I can get at least a lunch date with you by Friday."

"No, thank you. I'm not interested in dating right now."

"If I win, you have to go to the S.B. Carnival with me."

"I'm not going on a date with you." He won't win this bet. I've had my fill of bad boys and he's got heartbreaker written all over him.

"We're just going to lunch."

"No, we're not."

"Then it should be a safe bet," he teases.

"Fine, and when I win, you leave me alone."

"Deal." He grins at me when I crank up an Ozzy song on the radio. "You're going to be mine, Evie."

"Shut up and drive." The man is delusional.

The rest of our trip is pleasant enough, our discussions centering around music and T.V. shows. We have the same taste in entertainment. Mason sends a quick text when we get stuck at a red light.

"It's illegal to text and drive."

He regards me with a raised brow. "You going to turn me in?"

"Nah, then I'd have to drive home."

His phone beeps and he glances at the screen before tucking it in his pocket. "Looks like we have an hour to kill."

"What? Why?" I demand.

"Samuel won't be back at his store until one."

"Didn't he know we were coming?"

"He got called away. Relax, Evie. We'll find something to do," he says, smirking at me.

Fantastic. A few moments later, he pulls into a parking lot beside a small park. "I thought we could stretch our legs," he suggests, pointing to the narrow path winding away from the playground.

"Have you been here before?"

"A few years ago. The path leads back to a small stream. I'm going to grab a Coke." He gestures to the sub shop next door. "Want one?"

"Sure, thanks."

"I'll catch up with you." Christ, he looks good jogging away.

The air is filled with the laughter of children, the creak and clink of swings, backed by the dull roar of lunchtime traffic on the highway. A delicious mixture of scents from nearby restaurants makes my stomach growl. I shouldn't have skipped breakfast, but I didn't think I'd be running to BFE today.

The dirt path meanders along the perimeter of the park before leading me behind the tree line to a group of scarred picnic tables, shaded by a large oak tree. The sound of running water keeps me moving until I reach the stream. Clear water tumbles over a pile of smooth rocks and flows rapidly past the park, disappearing under a concrete slab of road in the distance. It's hot and humid today, and I'm really tempted to kick off my shoes and wade in. Yeah, right, and end up with an impetigo rash on my feet. Who knows what kind of runoff it's polluted with.

"Evie." His silky voice calls me. Why does he keep calling me that? Why the hell do I like it? The sun beams through the trees, spotlighting him like the damn Adonis he is as he wiggles a paper cup at me. "Hope you like Pepsi. All they had."

"Apparently not," I reply, glancing at the clear bag that houses two sub sandwiches and two bags of chips.

"Ah, well." For the first time, he seems a little unsure of himself. "I'm starving, and I didn't want to eat in front of you, so I got an extra sandwich. You don't have to eat it."

He's trying to be nice, and I can't be a bitch to him. "No, it's fine...I'm hungry. Thank you, but you have to let me pay you."

"Forget it. I'll just toss it in the creek." With an amused expression, he lays his food on the table and starts toward the creek with mine.

"What? No! Give it here!" He laughs as I try to snatch it from his hand.

"Say please," he teases, holding it above his head.

"Are you twelve?" Trying not to laugh, I return to the picnic table and unwrap his sandwich. His lips twitch up when I take a huge bite, chewing deliberately. Sitting across from me, he unwraps the second sandwich and opens a bag of potato chips, offering it to me.

"Thanks. I'll trade sandwiches if you want this one. I don't have cooties."

"Cooties? I thought I was the twelve year old, here?"

"Well, I suppose chasing you down for a sandwich wasn't exactly mature." I catch myself watching his lips as they wrap around the tip of his straw. They're so full and sexy. Am I seriously drooling over a man's lips?

"Maturity is overrated, and they're both roast beef, so no worries."

"It's good," I reply, taking another bite. "Tell me about yourself, Mason. What do you do other than stalk your volunteers?"

"I teach Mixed Martial Arts and I have my hand in a few other organizations. What about you? What do you do for fun?"

"For fun? Hang out with friends. Read. I have a book club meeting tonight."

He raises an eyebrow at me. "That's fun?"

"See. I'm totally boring and ordinary. Not your type at all. Aren't you relieved?"

Stuffing his sandwich wrapper in the bag, he replies, "You're not ordinary, love. Don't worry. I'll make sure you have fun on our date."

"You never give up, do you? Luckily, I think I've found you a date." I point to the tabletop where someone has scratched the words 'Tanya gives good head' deep into the wood. "She apparently performs oral well. I could write down the number for you."

Shaking his head, his amused eyes meet mine. "I won fair and square. You owe me. Are you reneging on our bet? You seemed more honorable. I'm truly disappointed, Evie."

Oh shit. We're eating lunch together. The bastard is smooth. "This isn't a lunch date!"

"A picnic lunch beside a babbling brook? This is the

ultimate lunch date, baby."

Ugh. This man is so frustrating! I ball up my trash, avoiding his gaze. "You tricked me."

"I don't remember getting any guidelines or rules. I got a lunch date with you. I win. We're going to the carnival together." A wide smile spreads across his face. Smug bastard.

"We're not."

"And then I'm taking you out to dinner."

"You don't understand the word 'No' do you?"

"Nothing wrong with my comprehension, love. Those gorgeous lips keep saying no, but those soft brown eyes are begging me not to give up."

"I'm not going to fuck you." That should send him running.

"I imagine the restaurant I have in mind would frown on that."

"I'm serious. I'm sure this approach normally works for you. That you can flash those baby blues, flex your muscles, and order girls into your bed. I'm telling you now, you have the wrong person. Stop wasting your time."

His rough hands catch mine, and he looks into my eyes. "Time is all we have, and there's never enough. Not a second spent with you would be a waste of time, Everly."

God, what his voice does to my name. "You only want me because I'm saying no."

"You're only saying no because you want me."

"You're deluded."

"You're beautiful. Now grab your trash. I can't date a litterbug."

Sighing, I shove my wrappers in the bag. "Just the carnival. That's all I agreed to. And save your charming little comments for someone more gullible."

"Ah, Evie." He slips an arm around my shoulder as we walk back to the van. "My baby blues, muscles, and charm. So many compliments from someone who isn't interested."

"You have a pretty broad definition of the word compliment."

"With you, I'll take what I can get."

We pull up to the small storefront just as a short dark skinned Latino man is unlocking the door. "Just in time, Reed. The shit's just inside," he calls. "Oh, hi, Miss. Sorry about the language. I didn't know Mason was bringing his girl," he explains with a sheepish smile.

"I'm a volunteer, not his girl, and don't worry, I've been known to drop an f-bomb or two."

"Hanging out with Mason will drive anyone to it." He laughs.

The truck is loaded in short order and we spend most of the ride home in comfortable silence. Mason gives me a sideways glance, grinning. "Don't pout."

"What? I'm not." Yeah, I sort of am. I can't believe how easily I fell for his trick.

"Is dating me that distasteful to you?"

Shit. I'm not trying to offend him. "Of course not. I'm just not interested in getting involved right now." After a few seconds of silence, I try to change the subject. "I saw a memo about a change to the S.B. carnival, but I didn't get to read it. What was it about?"

"I rented out Adventure River for the day since it's been so hot. The carnival will set up in the back lot."

He rented out the whole park? Adventure River is a huge waterpark complete with wave pool, lazy river, and massive water slides. "That's…fantastic. The kids will love it."

A small smile lifts his lips as he guides the car onto the highway off ramp. "You work with Building Tomorrow's Child, don't you? How many kids are in the center now?"

"Fifteen, why? And how do you know where I volunteer?"

"Background check, remember?"

"You're kind of a creepy stalker."

I get a flash of his straight white teeth as he laughs. "I'll get passes for the kids at the center. Bring them, but get the counselors to chaperone. I want you all to myself."

"Mason...that's...thank you. They'll be so excited."

"Not as excited as I am to see you in a swimsuit."

Damn, I hadn't thought of that. Oh, well, he's seen me naked. It's not like my chunky ass was hidden. When I look at him, I'm greeted with a wicked grin. "You're blushing."

"You're an asshole."

"I'll grow on you, love."

This time I can't help my laughter, and his eyes glitter with satisfaction. "My car is parked around back, if you'd just drop me there," I suggest as we pull up to Striking Back.

"In such a hurry to get rid of me," he jokes with a fake pout.

"I want to get to the gym before my book club meeting."

"Which gym do you go to?"

I unbuckle my belt as he parks beside my car. "No way, stalky. You have enough info on me at the moment."

"Fine. You don't need the gym, you know."

"You need an eye doctor."

"Hey." He grabs my arm as I open the van door. "Just don't overdo it on the elliptical. It'd be a shame to lose that ass." Oh my god.

"You're a Neanderthal."

"See you soon, Evie," he says with a smile. "Try not to think of me too much."

"I'll try to remember your name until the carnival." Without a backward glance, I hop out of the van and into my red Mini. All that linguistic sparring with him has worn me out. Damn, but the man is hard to resist. Charming, philanthropic, and too damn sexy to be real. He's also trouble. I know his type. Smooth words and a quick smile, and after he gets what he wants, on to the next leaving a mess of broken hearts behind him.

Ironically, he's what I would usually go for since I'm not looking for anything serious either. If he wasn't the owner of Striking Back, I'd probably give him a go, but there's no way I'm going to fuck him and then worry about running into him every week. S.B. is important to me, and I don't want to leave it behind for one night of sex, no matter how fantastic his ass is. So, it's settled. No sex with the tatted Adonis. The carnival is over a month away, and I'll come up with some excuse not to go with him.

After two hours at the gym, I stop by my apartment to shower before heading to my book club. We meet once a week in a small Italian restaurant downtown named Bellini's. It took me awhile to feel like I really fit in, but now, hanging out with these ladies is the highlight of my week. I know people picture a book club as a dry, boring meeting of bookworms, but we're far from it. There's no pretentious discussions of what the water imagery in a story represents while sipping coffee in a stuffy room.

The books we choose—when we actually read one—are typically the kind you want on your e-reader instead of in paperback, so no one can see the cover. Bellini's is owned by Marie's family and they reserve the back dining room for our boisterous group of fifteen wine guzzling, gossiping women. I love it.

"Ev!" Marie calls, as I make my way to an empty chair beside her. "You'll back me up on this." She gestures to Macy. "Best way to get over somebody is to get under somebody, am I right?" A grin settles on her face as she fills my wine glass.

"Oh, Macy, did you and Al break up?"

Macy's eyes glaze and she nods. "He's too controlling. I can't take it anymore. That alpha male shit may be hot in books, but in real life it sucks."

"You deserve better," I agree.

"He wants to tell me what to wear, who to talk to, where I can go. He's so jealous."

"I know it's hard now, but you're doing the right thing. Guys like that only get worse." Sometimes until they end up beating the shit out of the woman. "Look at you," I say with a grin, taking in her long straight ebony hair and almond shaped eyes. "You're gorgeous. The guys will be all over you when they find out you're single. Let him stick that up his jealous ass."

A wide smile spreads across her face and she gulps the last of her wine. "And Marie's not wrong," I add. "A little change of dick never hurt anybody." The room fills with laughter as Macy, Marie, and I clink our wine glasses together.

My phone chirps with a text message from an unfamiliar number.

-Having fun with your book club?-

Who the hell?

-Who is this?-

-You promised to remember my name until the carnival. I'm devastated.-

Mason. His stalker skills know no bounds. The bastard must've got to my phone when I wasn't watching.

-Do you invade everyone's privacy or am I special?-

-You're special. And I didn't look in your phone. Just used it to call mine.-

-Well, now I have your number, it's going on the bathroom wall.-

-You trying to get me a date?-

-Men's bathroom wall.-

-Ouch! I surrender.-

I can't help but smile, picturing his wicked grin.

-Good night Mason.-

-Good night Evie.-

"And who put that smile on your face?" Macy asks.

"What? Nobody."

Marie and Macy glance at each other before staring at me. "Spill it," Marie insists.

"He's infuriating, a stubborn Neanderthal. I didn't even give him my number! He swiped my phone to call his."

"Uh-huh. What's he look like?"

Sighing, I mumble, "Like a Greek God mated with a body building rock star."

"So what's the problem?" Macy asks.

"We sort of...work together." The table is filled with groans as the ladies nod in agreement.

"Run from that shit," Macy agrees.

"I know. I'm roped into this charity carnival thing with him. After that, no more contact."

"You sound like you're trying to convince yourself," Marie warns.

"Despite his caveman mentality, he's charming and fun, but I know better than to get involved with someone like him. I'm sure there's a trail of shattered hearts behind him."

"A playboy, huh?"

"Too gorgeous not to be."

Chapter Three

The jackhammer pounding away at my skull wakes me the next morning. That third glass of wine was a mistake. Before I can drag my hung over ass out of bed, there's a knock at my door. Great. It's not like I want to brush my teeth or shower before I face another human being.

"Who is it?" I ask, not recognizing the woman through the peephole.

"I have a delivery for Ms. Everly Hall from Mr. Reed."

Seriously? It's seven a.m. on a Saturday. The lady grins at me as if I don't look like death's grandmother. "Sorry to wake you, Ms. Hall, but Mr. Reed insisted I deliver these." A thick manila envelope is placed into my hand.

"Thank you," I mumble, but the woman is already halfway down the hall. Deciding the package can wait until I can see clearly, I head for the shower. My thoughts stray to Mason as I get cleaned up. It's not like I've never seen a hot guy before. I've had a few, but I always know where to draw the line.

Never sleep with someone who works with me, lives near me, or is a friend of a friend. It makes things too awkward when the inevitable end comes. Relationships are temporary and it's a hell of a lot easier to deal with that fact when you don't have to see that person again after it's over.

Dating Mason would be totally against my rules, but that doesn't stop me from thinking about him. I mean, maybe I could have him just once. I've never seen him before at S.B. and I've been there for months. Maybe it wouldn't be an issue. Yeah, this is me trying to find a loophole. I can't wait any longer to see what he sent me.

I dress quickly and towel dry my hair before flopping on the couch with the package. Evie is scrawled across the center of the envelope. Christ, even his handwriting is sexy. When I tear off the end, twenty day passes to Adventure River slide into my lap. He really sent passes for the kids! I'm confused by the twenty red paper wristbands I find next until I read the accompanying note.

Evie,

The wristbands are for unlimited rides at the carnival. Let me know if you need more. Remember to bring the other counselors. I want you all to myself for our date. I'll be thinking of you, beautiful.

How am I supposed to resist this? He's just arranged for fifteen underprivileged kids to spend a day at a waterpark and the evening at a carnival. Why is he doing this? To make sure I'll go? If so, it's working. I can't cancel now.

After a piece of toast and some orange juice, my head feels much better, and though it's not one of my usual days to volunteer at Building Tomorrow's Child, I can't wait to tell the kids. Danny, one of the boy's counselors, answers the phone when I call. "Hi, Danny, how's everything?"

"Just fine. Are you in today?"

"No, but I wanted to stop by. I have a surprise for the kids. Is it a good day?" Danny knows what I'm asking. There are a lot of challenges in running a group home, and that simple question encompasses a lot of others. Are there irate parents giving you shit? Are social workers or cops coming to inspect? Is one of the kids having a bad day?

"Everything's calm and peaceful, all things considered. Come on by. The kids will be glad to see you."

"On my way."

I can't resist stopping at a donut shop on my way. "Sweet tooth?" The elderly man behind the counter grins as he takes my order for four dozen donuts.

"Fifteen hungry kids," I reply with a laugh. "Half of them teenagers."

His eyes drift to my B.T.C. pin. "You work at the orphanage?"

"At the group home, yes, I volunteer."

"Well, aren't you a sweetheart." He gives me a wide smile. "I put an extra dozen glazed in there. I know how much a teenage boy can eat. Raised two of my own."

"Thank you. That's so kind. The boys will put them away," I reply, dropping a few bucks in the tip jar.

There are times when I get frustrated seeing how little the average person seems to care about the plight of their fellow humans. It's all about getting the next new phone or the latest tablet. Then I run into someone like the donut guy and I'm reminded the world is full of people who still care, who do what they can to help.

I'm mobbed by kids when I walk through the door of the group home. "Everly!" Justin cries, his skinny arms clamping around my waist.

"Hey, buddy! Are you having a good day?"

"Yep. Danny's going to let me pick tomatoes!"

"That'll be a hoot," James says, his sarcasm thick enough to trip over. At fifteen years old, he's our resident complainer.

"That sounds fun, Justin. Let's go have a donut first, what do you say?"

"Yay!" All the kids cheer and follow me to the dining room. Two of the older girls pass out napkins and pour cups of orange juice.

After all the kids are settled and eating, Danny pops in and snatches a chocolate covered donut. "Sure, Ev, sugar them up and leave them with me," he says with a smile.

"Just thought I'd make your day more interesting. Where's Monica?" I ask, looking around for the girl's counselor.

"Took Geneva to the eye doctor. They should be back soon."

"Okay, guys, settle down. I have a surprise for you," I announce.

"Our parents aren't really worthless assholes who don't want us?" James says.

"My mom wants me!" Justin cries.

"Real nice, James," Amber scolds, hugging Justin.

"There's a carnival coming up and everyone is invited. I have a wristband for each of you, so you can ride as many rides as you want."

A cheer goes up as the kids start firing questions. "Will there be bumper cars? Can I get cotton candy? Are you going with us?"

"I don't know exactly what rides they'll have, but I think cotton candy is a safe bet. I might see you there, but I won't be chaperoning. Quiet down because I haven't told you the best part. The carnival is being held behind Adventure River Waterpark, and a…friend of mine has rented the park for the day. You're all going. They have a wave pool and lots of fun waterslides."

"What's the catch?" James asks, his face wary. "This some church group? We gotta get right wit Jay-sus to get in?"

"James," Danny growls.

Truthfully, I don't blame James for being suspicious. When good things don't happen to you very often, you always look for the downside when they do. "The catch is you have to smile and have fun. And wear sun block," I add with a grin.

The kids are ecstatic. Between their excitement and the sugar, there's no keeping them indoors. As they run around the backyard, playing on the recently installed playground equipment, Danny and I relax on the picnic table. “So, how did you manage this?” Danny asks, his light blond curls dancing in the wind.

“The day is being hosted by Striking Back. They know I also volunteer here, so they offered.”

“That’s fantastic. You don’t want to chaperone?”

“I can’t, but I’ll be there.” Danny stares at me, confused. In the two years I’ve known him, he’s asked me out at least ten times. I’ve always told him the truth, I don’t date people I work with, but it hasn’t stopped him from trying. “I have a date,” I admit, grudgingly.

“Well, don’t sound so happy about it.” He laughs.

“It’s a long story, but I’ll see you guys there.” As if he knows I’m thinking of him, my phone chimes.

-Good morning, love-

Oh, somebody help me.

-Good morning. I got the passes and wristbands. The kids are so excited. Thanks so much!-

An idea strikes me and I call for the kids. Danny helps me wrangle them and a few minutes later, I text Mason a picture of the group with Thank You Mr. Reed written across the bottom.

-They’re very welcome. You have your hands full today.-

-Not today. Just stopped by to share the good news.-

-Good. You’ll have plenty of time to prepare for our date tonight.-

Ha, nice try.

-I think you need to check the calendar. Our date is weeks away.-

-Far too long. I want to see you.-

-Sorry, have to pass.-

-Do you have a date, Evie?-

-With my couch and a new book.-

-Let me guess, a romance? I can give you romance.-

Uh, huh, until the moment he comes. It’s time to mess with him.

-Sort of a romance book, I guess, if you call bondage and spanking romance.-

-You just made me hard at work. I'll see you at seven.-

Stubborn arrogant jackass.

-No, you won't. Not tonight.-

-Talk to you later, beautiful.-

Ugh! This man is so irritating! Sweet, but stubborn as hell. I'm not going out with him tonight. Absolutely not.

The knock at the door sounds at exactly seven o'clock. That arrogant bastard. I told him no! He can't just order me on a date. Screw him. I'm not opening the door. "Evie, I'll sit here all night. Open up."

A few seconds later, I hear Charlotte, my elderly neighbor, call out, "Everly? You okay, sweetie?" Shit Shit Shit. Now I have to open the door or make a scene.

Mason's amused look when I yank open the door makes me want to punch him in the throat. Instead, I force a smile. "I'm fine, Charlotte, thank you." She grins and heads back into her apartment. "Come in," I grumble.

"I'd love to." That damn smirk. His eyes travel over my sweats. "Not that you don't look lovely in anything, but the restaurant may have a bare minimum of a dress code."

"I told you I'm not going out with you. And I've already eaten," I add, gesturing to the pizza box on the table.

"We don't have to go to dinner. Just let me take you out. I have something very special I want to show you."

I'll bet he does. He laughs when my eyes involuntarily dart to his crotch. "Not that special, although I'm happy to arrange a viewing of that as well."

"I'll pass on both."

"Are you always this stubborn?"

"Are you always this persistent?"

"Only when I really want something." I'm overwhelmed by his spicy masculine scent when he steps closer to me, resting his hand on my shoulder. "Give me two hours, Evie. If you don't have fun, I'll never bother you again." His hand slides up my neck and pulls the band from my hair, letting it fall to my shoulders. Warm breath bathes my ear, his lips hovering a centimeter away while he whispers, "Come with me, Evie."

Damn. It. All. "Give me ten minutes," I murmur, surrendering to him. It's either go out with him or strip him right here. Either way, I know how this will end. I'd be lying if I said I wasn't looking forward to climbing this man like a tree.

After a quick change into jeans, a red long sleeved blouse, and black converse sneakers, I run the straightener through my hair a few times and call it good. Showing up like this, he's lucky I don't go in pajamas.

"You'll need a jacket, love," he says with a smile that makes me want to take all these clothes right back off. "It's chilly." I grab my jacket, and he takes my hand as I lock the door. "I'm parked down the street," he tells me, keeping hold of my hand while we walk. I expect a sports car, the sort that screams playboy or mid-life crises, so I'm surprised when he opens the passenger door of a dark mid-sized sedan. A satisfied smile settles on his face as he pulls into the flow of traffic.

"Alright, you've got me in your car. Where are we going?"

"It's a surprise."

"Your surprise better not include a bed." Because I don't have the willpower to say no.

"Well, damn, I'll have to think of something else." He glances at me when I take out my phone. "What are you doing?"

"Setting my alarm for two hours." I can't help but grin when his laughter fills the car. When he lays his hand on my knee, I don't hesitate to cover it with mine. We pull into the empty parking lot of the Indianapolis Zoo and he smiles at the confusion on my face. "Is this where you plan to dump my body? Because White River's probably a better option."

"And waste a body like that? Never." He parks at the front of the dim lot and hurries to open my door for me. I wonder if he's the gentlemanly type in bed as well? "Do you like animals?"

"Of course."

"What's your favorite animal?" He wraps his arm around my shoulders as we walk toward the darkened entrance. "Bonobo's, but Mason, it's closed. They won't let us in."

"I donate to their cause, plus a friend of mine works here. He'll meet us at the gate. A bonobo is a monkey, right?"

"A chimp. They're our closest relatives."

"Reed! About damn time." A thin blond man greets us at the gate. "Come on back."

Mason nods at his friend. "Larry, this is Evie, my date."

Larry grins and shakes my hand. "Poor girl. Would you like me to lock him up so you can escape? Call you a cab?"

"Not yet, but I'll keep it in mind." Mason shakes his head, and I laugh. "I like your friend."

"Watch it, baby," he growls, pulling us hip to hip.

We follow Larry along a dimly lit path through the exhibits until he stops. "You're just in time to feed him," he says, unlocking a heavy metal door.

Feed what? What am I walking into? It suddenly occurs to me I don't really know either of these men. They could be leading me into a tiger's cage. Mason squeezes my hand when I retreat. "Feed what?"

"Oh, nothing dangerous, Miss. He's just a baby."

Mason wraps an arm around me, and I lean into his warmth. "I wouldn't put you in danger, love. Trust me."

Nodding, I allow them to lead me inside. Just a baby, he said, but a baby what? Baby monkey, fine. Baby tarantula or alligator, not so much. When we round the corner, I freeze at the sight of a full grown panda asleep behind a wall of glass.

Larry shakes his head and says, "She's sedated, poor thing. She's ill and hasn't been able to nurse her cub."

"Will she live?"

"I hope so." Larry disappears behind a partition.

Mason runs his thumb along my jaw as I stare at the beautiful sleeping bear. "Are you okay?"

"Yes, she's beautiful," I exclaim, moving closer to the glass. "I've never seen a panda. I heard a zoo in Georgia has one, but..."

"Yes, this is only temporary and the public won't see

them," Larry says, returning with a bundle wrapped in a gray blanket. "Tomorrow they'll be moved to an animal hospital where they're better equipped to care for them."

My heart stops when he pulls back the edge of the blanket to reveal a tiny white and black fuzz ball. "Oh! So adorable!"

"He's six weeks old so his fur is starting to come in. He can't see or stand yet, not for another two months or so." Tiny cries emanate from the little creature. "He's hungry," Larry says, producing a bottle. "Would you like to feed him?"

"Feed him? I want to take him home," I reply as he gently rests the bundled cub in my arms. Mason leads me to a small sofa and sits beside me while I put the bottle to the cub's mouth. After a second, he latches on, and I laugh with delight.

The click of Mason's cell phone camera makes me look up. "You'll want to remember this," he says with a soft smile.

"Look at him. Isn't he the most beautiful thing?" I run my fingers through the silky fur on the cub's belly.

"Almost," Mason replies with a grin, and I feel a blush climb my cheeks. I'm in so much trouble.

The little guy falls asleep by the end of the bottle, and I'm able to spend a few minutes just holding him. His fur is thin and downy soft under my fingers. This is one of those things I know I'll remember for the rest of my life. The average person doesn't ever see a panda outside of a T.V. screen, and I held one, fed him. It's an amazing experience.

"I should put him back in the incubator," Larry says. "We have to keep him warm."

"Of course." I reluctantly hand him over. "Thank you so much for letting me visit."

"You're welcome. I'm glad you could see him." Larry returns the baby panda to its bed and walks us out the door.

"So," Mason teases with a grin. "Want to go hold the snakes before we leave?"

"Sure, I had a five foot ball python when I was a kid."

"Of course you did." He laughs. "Is there anything you're afraid of?"

Right now? Him, but there's no way I'm admitting that.

"Spiders."

"Ugh. I'm in total agreement."

Larry says goodbye to us at the gate, and Mason tucks me against his side as we walk to the car. He's so warm, I can't help but lean into him, and he drops a quick kiss on my temple. "Well, did I keep my part of the bargain? Did you have fun?"

We stop beside the car, and I slip my arms around his waist. "That was amazing. I'll never forget it. Thank you for bringing me, for showing me something so rare and special."

"Like you," he murmurs, sliding his hand into my hair to cup my head.

"Are you comparing me to a panda?" I whisper, my breath catching as his gaze drops to my lips.

"Rare and special," he murmurs, his mouth grazing softly across mine with the softest of kisses. "My panda."

Who the hell could resist this man? When his soft lips press firmly against mine, every inch of my body tingles. My skin flushes with heat as he takes my mouth with his, nibbling and sucking. His hands cup my face while his tongue flicks between my lips.

A small moan escapes me when he deepens the kiss. I don't know how long we stand there, exploring and tasting. Time seems to have no meaning when I'm in this man's arms. "Come home with me," he says when we break the kiss. "I promise I'll make it good, Everly."

God, I love how he says my name. "Are you promising I'll have fun?" I tease.

"Time of your life, love." My phone alarm blares and he gives me a crooked smile. "I'll need more than two hours this time."

I expect an apartment or condo downtown, so I'm surprised when we head north of the city. "You live in the suburbs?"

"Not exactly. I like my privacy. No close neighbors to hear you scream my name." I shake my head at him, but can't help the grin on my face.

"I hate to disappoint you, but I'm not a screamer."

"I take that as a challenge."

We pull into a gated community, and he stops to enter a code at the gate, waving to the security guard as we pass through. The neat streets are lined with two and three story houses, all well spaced and immaculate. I can almost smell the money. How does he afford this? I can't imagine owning a charity brings in much.

"What do you do? I mean other than Striking Back?"

"I teach Mixed Martial Arts a couple days a week."

That explains that body. All those muscles, soft-hearted, and he can fight. I feel my panties trying to pull themselves down. "Did you ever fight professionally?"

He looks at me like I'm trying to trick him. "Are you serious?"

"Sorry, I just thought if you taught, maybe you used to fight."

"I did. I retired a few years ago. Now I teach, help train the next generation of fighters," he replies, pulling into a circular driveway at the end of a cul-de-sac. A large two story brick home looms large in the dark.

"I can actually see stars out here," I remark with a grin as he leads me to his front door.

"I like being outside the city, away from all the noise and pollution."

"Me, too. I love the country."

"Make yourself at home," he says, leading me into his living room. "I'll start a fire."

I take a seat on his long black sectional couch, and my eyes don't leave his body as he squats to arrange the logs in the fireplace. His shirt rides up, showing a bare strip of skin above his jeans, and I wonder if he's a boxer or briefs man. If it's boxer briefs, I'm going to lose it. After lighting the fire, he heads toward the kitchen. "Would you like something to drink?"

"Water, please."

When he returns, he hands me a bottle of water and places another on the coffee table. "So, you like the outdoors? Do you like to camp?"

"Love it. I just got back from a camping trip with the kids from BTC. Fishing, swimming in the lake, roasting marshmallows. We had a blast."

"A girl after my own heart," he says with a grin. That's not what I'm after tonight. Being this close to him, I can barely control the urge to rip his clothes off and lick those bulging muscles. "Tell me you made smores."

"Huh?" Shit. I was staring at his ass instead of listening.

He sits on the edge of the couch and reaches to brush a strand of hair off my cheek. "You were checking me out. Are you happy with what you see?" His deep voice is teasing.

"Not too shabby."

"Well, if you can ignore my shabby ass a moment, I asked if you had smores on your last camping trip."

Pull it together, Everly! I'm making a fool of myself drooling over him. I can't explain it. I mean, he's sexy, but it's more than that. I just want him. "Nope. Forgot the graham crackers, and I really wanted to try them."

"You've never had smores?" When I shake my head, he abruptly rises, jogs to the kitchen, and returns with a long wooden skewer, a bag of marshmallows, a bag of mini Hershey bars, and a stack of graham crackers. "We're correcting this travesty right now."

"Well, aren't you the boy scout?"

"Always prepared," he agrees, tugging me to sit beside him on the floor. He impales a marshmallow and hands me the skewer. Pressing his body close to mine, he says, "The trick is to keep it in the heat, not the flame."

His warm hand lands over mine on the skewer and positions the marshmallow where he wants it. I really hope he doesn't see the goose bumps running up my arm. The guy just touched my hand and I'm losing it. We watch until the marshmallow turns a golden brown, and he pulls it from the fire before handing me two graham crackers topped with chocolate. I squeeze the marshmallow between the crackers and pull it off the skewer.

When I offer it to him first, he takes the dripping treat and holds it to my lips, watching as I take a bite and lick the gooey marshmallow from the corner of my mouth.

"Good?"

"Delicious. Kind of messy." My hand is caught halfway to my face when I try to wipe a drip of chocolate from my bottom lip. My gaze meets his a split second before his tongue flutters across my lip, licking away the chocolate. Shit. Did I just moan? Seriously? That was so hot.

"Evie," he breathes. "I can't wait another second to have you." Before I can think of a response, his lips are on mine and any chance at cognizant thought is long gone. His kiss is different this time. Possessive and insistent. He's dominating my mouth and I'm loving every second.

I feel his smile when I slide my hands beneath his shirt, my fingers tracing the hard lines of his stomach muscles. I want to lick them.

"Your skin is so soft," he whispers, running his hand up and down my spine before unfastening my bra. "And you smell amazing." I tug his shirt off, and he returns the favor, letting my bra fall off my chest to the floor. "So beautiful." He's looking at my B-cups like he's hit the lottery.

Streaks of pleasure shoot through me when his thumbs skim over my nipples, making them pebble with the slightest touch. I've never been so turned on in my life. I grab his lips with mine, kissing him long and deep. I'm indulging in one night with this man, and I'm going to lick every inch of his sweaty muscled body. With a growl—I swear the man growled—he picks me up and carries me to his bedroom, pausing to turn on the light.

I'm placed on the bed and his hot mouth is on my breast before I can move, his fingers unfastening my jeans. When I unbutton his pants, he backs up and pulls my jeans and panties off, desire burning in his eyes as they travel over me. "No fair," I whisper, as he stands over my bare body. "Show me yours."

A chuckle rattles his chest. "Oh, I'll show you mine, love. After I look at you, taste you. I've been picturing this for so long. I have to savor it." Again, I have no response, just picturing that face between my legs has struck me mute.

Piercing eyes meet mine and a fiendish grin makes my heart race as he drops to his knees and tugs me to the edge of the bed. "You're a lot less argumentative in bed. I'll have to remember that next time you wag that sharp tongue at me." I turn my head, unable to meet his eyes when he spreads my legs and gazes between them.

"Turn the light off," I order, feeling way too vulnerable.

"Not a chance, sweetheart." A soft fingertip runs through my folds, tracing them lazily. "You're pretty here, too."

"Oh, God," I groan as he slips a thick finger into me, circling and teasing. Wet, open mouthed kisses burn a trail from the inside of my knee, up my inner thigh until I feel his hot breath between my legs. Ice blue eyes peek up at me, the crooked smile on his face telling me I'm in trouble.

He doesn't start slow. I nearly scream when his tongue dives inside, then covers every inch of me in seconds. He eats me ravenously, making me fight to close my legs, to control the sensations that are too much, too strong. Thick arms clamp around my thighs, holding me open to his devastating mouth and I plead, "Mason."

His responding hum vibrates against me, and I moan again. He latches on just above my opening and sucks at me, sending fire shooting through my core as every nerve ending I possess stands at attention. "Oh! Fuck!"

Just before I come, he slows and moves down to drag his tongue everywhere but where I need it. "No, please," I whimper, trying to pull him back where I need him. Just another few seconds.

I feel his smile. "In good time, baby. We've got all night."

Not if I choke him to death with my thighs. He left me hanging on purpose. He takes his time lapping at me, stroking in and out with his fingers, keeping me right on the edge while I squirm and pant.

"Mason," I groan.

"Does it feel good?" Good doesn't begin to describe it.

"Too good. Please."

"I love to hear you beg for me."

"You've got about ten seconds before I kick you in the balls."

He throws his head back, laughing. "I've got you, baby." He trails his lips up and seals his mouth over my clit, sucking slow and steady, ignoring my hands trying to tear out his hair. I'm drowning in pleasure, making noises that barely sound human. My world tilts and shatters, leaving me in a freefall I never want to end. He lessens the pressure, stroking over me with the flat of his tongue, making the spasms go on and on.

When I finally gain control, he's standing at the edge of the bed, grinning down at me and taking off his pants. Boxer briefs! And they hug every delicious inch of him. Speaking of inches. When he shoves down the underwear, I try not to react to the python that's pointed at me, but Christ, he's huge. I've never been with a man that big.

His smile widens at my expression, and he rolls a condom over the beer can he calls a cock before crawling up my body. "I'll go easy," he says, planting a long soft kiss on my lips.

"Kind of explains your arrogance."

"You're just mad because I made you scream."

"Yeah, please, never do that again." He chuckles, and I feel him nudging at my entrance, ending my attempt at humor.

"Sorry, not going to be able to do it. That was sexy as hell. I need to hear it again."

I bury my face in his neck with a gasp as he slides halfway in. His brow furrows in concentration while he rocks slowly in and out, plunging deeper with each stroke until he's buried in me. I feel stretched to the limit, crammed full of him and it's too damn good.

"You okay, love?"

"Yes," I moan, tilting my hips to meet his.

"Oh, Fuck, Evie." True to his word, he takes his time, fucking me with slow deliberate strokes. Pushing and dragging through swollen, sensitive tissues until I'm building again.

"I'm going to come," I gasp, thrusting against him. He obliges, giving it to me harder and faster until I fall apart beneath him, my hands clawing his firm ass. His rhythm falters and he groans my name as he comes.

Goddamn it. I knew he'd be good.

Thin sunlight bleeds through the drapes, throwing just enough light for me to see where the hell I am. Shit. I spent the night. I didn't mean to do that. After our second time where I rode him like a feral horse, he crashed hard. I meant to let him sleep a few, then call a cab, but I guess he wore me out.

My phone shows it's only five a.m. so maybe I can still avoid the awkward morning after where we fill each other with lies about how we'll call. As I dress, I take a second to appreciate the human work of art spread out before me. He looks young and vulnerable in sleep, his long eyelashes fanned over his cheeks. God, the beauty of the eyes behind those eyelids is something to remember.

With that stubbly jawline and muscled body, he's far too masculine to be described with the word beautiful. His arms are tucked behind his head, his biceps bulging. I have a wonderful memory of squeezing them as I rode him the night before, and the look on his face when he came was the thing of fantasies. My vibrator is going to think its name is Mason.

This is my chance to get a better look at the colorful tattoos that sleeve his right arm and dip to cover half his chest. Deep green vines and leaves wind around his bicep and grow across his chest. Scattered between them are drawings of different flowers. I recognize a few. Pastel yellow magnolias, purple hyacinths, bright red gladiolus. They're beautiful, detailed, and truly a work of art, but it's a little odd for a man to get tats of flowers, isn't it? Flaming skulls and big tittied women seem more their style.

In the dip between his clavicle and neck, there's an outline or maybe a scar. It's so faint I can't tell. I jump when he snorts and rolls onto his side. I need to quit ogling him and get out of here before he wakes up.

I find my shirt on the living room floor beside his. The half-eaten smore lies near the fireplace, and I consider throwing it away, but I want him to see it, to remember me. Which reminds me, I need my souvenir.

It's weird and creepy, I know, but I've done it as long as I can remember. When I was moved from one foster home to another, I always took something to remember them, and left something so they'd remember me. After a quick glance around the room, I pick up his shirt and stuff it in my purse. Now I can go.

I step outside before calling Yellow Cab, and spend fifteen minutes waiting at the edge of the road until it shows up. The driver gives me a knowing smile. Catching a cab at five-thirty a.m. on a Sunday with mussed hair and wrinkled clothes is a blatant walk of shame announcement. I get the same look from the people in the lobby of my apartment building, and though I try really hard, I can't find a shit to give. After a quick shower, I fall into bed and back to sleep.

The buzzing of my phone wakes me a few hours later, and the display shows I've missed two calls and a few texts. Mason? Why is he calling already? I didn't leave anything behind.

The first text is from Ian.

-Get your ass up. Have lunch with me today.-

The last three are Mason.

-Is there a reason I woke to an empty bed?-

The next is time stamped an hour later.

-What the hell, Evie?-

And another hour later.

-Call me, Everly.-

What does he want? Guys never like to wake up to a one night stand, and I spared him the experience. He should be grateful. I don't want to talk to him, so I settle for texting him.

-Sorry, had to be somewhere. Had fun. Hope you did too. Thanks for a wonderful night.-

My phone beeps almost instantly.

-You had to be somewhere before six a.m. on Sunday? I call bullshit.-

He must've woke just after I left.

-Didn't want to overstay my welcome. Last night was great. Talk to you later.-

-Quit trying to ditch me and ANSWER YOUR PHONE.-

I've barely read his text when my phone buzzes again. Persistent asshole. I relent and press the accept call button. "It's rude to use all caps, you know."

"Why didn't you feel welcome?" he demands.

"What? I didn't mean…look, we both know how this goes. I didn't want you to wake, realize I spent the night and worry I'd try to stay and make breakfast or something."

"I don't know who you've been dating, Evie, but he's obviously an asshole. I wouldn't have asked you here if I didn't want you to stay, and not just until we're done in bed. Next time, I want breakfast."

Next time? "You still want me to go to the carnival with you?"

He sighs. "You promised me the carnival, but that's not the next time I have in mind."

"Mason, I'm sorry if I upset you by leaving, and I'll go to the waterpark and carnival, but I'm really not looking for anything else right now."

"It's when you aren't looking that you find what's missing, Panda. I'll call you later. Have a good day."

He hangs up before I can reply, leaving me thoroughly confused and frustrated.

Chapter Four

"So what do you think he wants?" I ask Ian as he steals a french fry from my plate.

"You," he replies simply.

"You aren't helping."

"Ev, the guy is obviously trying like hell to spend time with you. He took you on a fantastic date, fucked your brains out, then got upset when you snuck out. He's way into you. Most girls would be planning the wedding."

He grins when I roll my eyes at him. "And I'm so like most girls."

"You want my advice? Quit analyzing it to death. A hot guy wants you and you're looking for the catch. You're the catch, girl, a great one. Give the guy a chance and have some fun." Ian tips a wink at the pretty red headed waitress who refills our drinks, and she smiles at him.

"Remind me why I'm taking dating advice from you," I scoff, taking his glass and drinking the last of his Coke.

"Because I have so much experience."

A couple walks past us, arms linked around one another, staring at each other like they're the only people in the world. The stab of jealousy I feel is quickly followed by pity for them. They're so wrapped up in each other now, so happy, but eventually it'll come back to bite them.

"If the woman you took home left after you fell asleep, how

would you feel?"

His dark eyes meet mine, his smile reluctant. "Relieved."

"See, that's what I was going for."

"So you're looking for a guy like me? Who takes a different girl home every week?"

"I'm not looking for a guy at all. But Mason doesn't seem to hear the word No, and when we're face to face, I have a hard time turning him down."

The perky waitress returns to check on us. If she bats her eyelashes any faster she's going to take flight. "Can I get you anything else?"

"A slice of apple pie, please, alamode," I order, falling back on my belief that junk food cures anything.

"Can I get you anything?" Ms. Perky asks Ian.

He hands her his cell phone. "Would you fix this for me? There's something wrong with it."

A confused look creases her face as she looks at his phone. "Doesn't look broken."

"It's missing your number, which makes it totally useless to me. I may as well throw it away." Ian kicks me under the table when I shake my head, trying to not to laugh.

With a blush and a giggle, she enters her name and number in his contacts, smiling from ear to ear. When she walks away to retrieve my pie, Ian returns to our conversation without missing a beat. "Look, Ev, you're scared. After what happened with Sean, I get it. You've dated plenty of guys since him, but this is the first time you've talked about someone like this. You like him."

I flop back in my chair. "He got in my head."

Ian snatches my fork and steals the first warm bite of pie when it's placed in front of me. "He got in more than that." He laughs, cocking an eyebrow. "Can he fuck?"

"Like a champ."

"So, he's gorgeous, well off, good in bed, and totally into you. I'm so sorry you have to suffer the indignity of being pursued by such a guy."

"Well, now I just sound like a bitch."

His eyes soften, and he reaches to squeeze my hand. "No,

Ev. You've been screwed over too many times by too many people. You're scared because you like him and you don't want to get hurt again. We screw up our relationships in different ways, but underneath our reasons are the same."

No one understands better than Ian the damage done by a childhood in the system. Having countless people claim to care for you, even love you, until you make a mistake. Then it's on to the next one, never knowing where you'll end up, only that you'll be alone. Everything is temporary and out of our control.

"I just don't want you to run away from every chance at happiness," Ian adds.

Nodding, I take a drink of my lemonade to wash down the lump in my throat. "I want the same for you."

"If I meet someone half as good as you, I'll give her a chance." His mischievous smile makes me grin. "Until then, I'm going to nail this waitress who keeps picturing me naked."

"Who said romance is dead?" I laugh.

"It's no date to bottle feed a panda, but she'll enjoy it," he teases, leaning to hug me. He drops a twenty on the table. "Be good, pup. Love ya."

"Love ya."

Thankfully, the next week is uneventful compared to the hectic one before. Mason and I text each other a few times, and I have to admit, I like the back and forth. My phone wakes me early Friday morning, and Danny chuckles at my mumbled hello.

"Ev? I'm sorry to wake you, but we have a situation here today. Monica has a family emergency and Stacy can't come in until three. Can you please help us out?"

"Be there in an hour."

"You're the best."

"I'm aware. You better have coffee."

At least I'm able to beat the rush hour traffic. I arrive at Building Tomorrow's Child just as the older kids are leaving for school. "Thank God for you, Ev. Ally is home with a cold. She's asleep in her room, but we need to watch her fever. We also have a new boy who arrived last night, and he needs some one on one time, which is hard to do with two wild four year olds running around." He eyes the twins who are fighting over an action figure.

"I'll keep an eye on Ally and hang out with the new boy."

"His name is Matthew and he's pretty upset. His parents were busted growing a few pot plants. They took him straight out of his bed yesterday morning. On his eighth birthday, no less."

"Poor kid. I'll talk to him." The ridiculous pot laws in our state separate more children from their parents than actual abuse. While other states are decriminalizing marijuana, or at least reducing the penalty to a fine, Indiana has clamped down.

Offenders who are caught growing can get a year in prison for each plant. They're charged with intent to distribute, whether or not they're actually selling it. I've seen some get more time than child molesters, rapists, and murderers. Where's the justice in that?

While Danny takes the twins out to play, I settle on the small sofa beside Matthew. He's curled up against the arm, staring blankly at a commercial on television. "Can I watch with you?" I'm rewarded with a small nod. "My name is Everly, but everyone calls me Ev. Should I call you Matthew, or do you like Matt better?"

"Matty," he whispers.

"I'm happy to meet you, Matty. I'm sorry to see you so sad, though. Do you want to talk about it?"

"Drug dealers are bad people," he says, turning to regard me with a miserable look. "My teacher said so."

"I don't think that's true, Matty. Everyone makes mistakes. It doesn't mean they're bad."

"My mommy and daddy aren't bad. I wanna go home," he wails, and I pull him into my lap, rocking him and letting him cry. Sometimes, it's all you can do. These kids break my heart in a thousand different ways.

"I'll never see them again."

I turn him to face me. Pale green eyes gaze into mine, pleading for me to make it all better. "Listen to me, Matty. You'll see your mom and dad again. I know this is scary and you feel like you're all alone, but it'll get better. You aren't alone."

"When can I go home?"

"I don't know, honey. It isn't up to me. A judge has to say

it's okay first. Until that happens, Danny, Monica, and the other counselors will take good care of you. If you're hurt or scared, or just bored, you can go to them."

He scoots off my lap and scrubs the tears off his cheek. "What about you?"

"I'm not here every day, but we'll be able to hang out if you want. Danny said you didn't eat dinner or breakfast. Are you hungry?" He shrugs, staring at the carpet. "Do you like pancakes?"

"Mommy makes them on Saturday mornings."

"I'll bet your mom's a good cook."

A tiny smile cracks through the despair. "She is. She was going to make me a birthday cake, but..." His lip trembles.

"I'm sure your mom will make you the best cake ever when you get home. I know it won't be the same as your mom's, but I make a pretty good cake, especially if I have some help." I grin at him, and his smile widens.

"Can we?"

"After we have some breakfast, okay?"

"Okay."

When Danny brings the twins in for lunch, Matty is sitting at the counter with chocolate batter smeared across his mouth as he licks the beater. "Something smells good," Danny remarks.

"Birthday cake!" Matty exclaims.

"Awesome. Do I get a piece?"

"Sure." Matty grins up at him. "Hope you like it crunchy."

Danny's confused expression makes me laugh. "We may have lost a chunk of eggshell in the mix."

Danny ruffles Matty's hair and says, "I like crunchy. How about you go wash your hands and face before lunch?"

"Okay." Matty hops off the stool and follows the twins to the restroom.

"Ev, you're a lifesaver. He needed you."

"He just needed someone to talk to."

Danny moves beside me as I'm washing the dishes. He's so close his hip is touching mine. "No, he needed you. You have a way with these kids. You should become a counselor."

"I appreciate the thought, but I enjoy working with my

other charity as well. I couldn't give either of them up." His warm hands fall on my shoulders, rubbing. "Danny, we've talked about this," I warn, drying my hands on a dishtowel.

He grabs my arms as I turn around. "Go out with me Friday night."

"No, I told you, I'm not looking for..." My words are interrupted when his lips land on mine. Have you ever kissed your own hand? Yeah, that's pretty much what it felt like. Just blah, nothing. I step away from him seconds before the kids charge back into the room.

With a satisfied grin I'd like to remove with a ball of steel wool, he turns to face the fridge. "I'll make lunch."

My phone buzzes with a new text as I return to the living room with the kids. After finding a rerun of Spongebob they all agree on, I'm able to slip away a moment.

-What are you making me for dinner tonight?-

I can't help but smile at the sight of Mason's name. The way he kissed me sure wasn't blah. I swear I can still taste him, and just the thought sends tingles racing across my skin.

-Sorry, sir, you must have the wrong number.-

-So this isn't my beautiful brunette spitfire who lives to be difficult?-

His beautiful brunette? Maybe he really does have the wrong number.

-Nope, sorry, no one like that here. Just a run of the mill woman with a top notch bullshit detector.-

-I like Italian. Seven o'clock okay?-

Goddamn it, here we go again. Despite his caveman antics, I realize I'm dying to see him again. We have a few weeks until the carnival, maybe I can just see him until then, get him out of my system, and then we can end it. Keep in mind it's temporary, and nobody gets hurt or used. Well, I suppose technically we're using each other, but I can live with that. He's spectacular in bed.

-I suppose I can make a lasagna.-

-Wow, you gave in so easy. Are you day drinking?-

-Did you just call me easy? Not drinking yet, but I'm sure I'll need a bottle to get through the evening.-

-You're the opposite of easy.-

-Hard?-

-Yes, I am, thinking about your legs wrapped around my neck.-

Christ, I love his dirty talk.

-I believe we agreed on lasagna.-

-I'm having you for dessert. See you at seven, Panda.-

I hope I'm not making a mistake. Ian's advice flows through my mind. Relax, have fun. Mason is definitely fun. In bed and out. His insistent pestering is annoying, but I admit I'm flattered. He can have his choice of women, but he's annoying me.

Danny calls the kids for lunch and after getting them settled, approaches me in the living room. "Ev…"

I hold up my palm, interrupting him. "That can't happen again."

"I didn't mean to do that here, you know, where the kids might see."

"It can't happen anywhere. I'm…seeing someone," I mumble. Mason and I are nowhere near exclusive, but I'm sure going to use him to my advantage now.

"Really?" He looks doubtful, which just pisses me off. Like I owe him an explanation.

"Yes, really."

"What's his name?"

"Not that it's any of your business, but it's Mason Reed."

If his jaw drops any farther, he'll trip over it. "Mason Reed, the fighter?"

"He doesn't fight anymore. He teaches MMA."

"You're dating the former middleweight champion?" His eyes darken and he scrubs his palm across his cheek. "Shit. Don't tell him I kissed you."

My laugh comes out as a snort. "No worries there. I'm going to frost Matty's cake and then head out."

He nods and leaves me to it. I'm on my way home when I get a text from him.

-Matty's disappointed you won't be here when we sing happy birthday and cut the cake.-

Shit. I should be there. I'll just have to make it a late dinner with Mason.

-What time?-

-Seven-

-I'll be there.-

I decide not to be chickenshit and call Mason instead of texting. He picks up on the second ring. "Hi, Evie." Oh, his voice does terrible things to me.

"Hey, listen, I'm sorry, but I have to be at BTC for a last minute birthday party tonight."

"Are you trying to ditch me? I'm catching a pattern here."

"No! We could meet later tonight, if you want."

"Are you turning this into a booty call?" I can hear the amusement in his voice as he teases me.

"I'm sorry, are you too sophisticated for such behavior?"

"Not normally, but I was really looking forward to that lasagna. I'll take you to the birthday party and then we'll have dinner before I show you my qualifications rank me far above booty call material, love. What time should I pick you up?"

I nearly drop the phone at his suggestion. "You want to go to an eight year old's birthday party?"

"I want to spend time with you. Wherever." His tone is serious. My brain is screaming at me to put an end to this right now. He's either trying to play me, or he's looking for more, which he won't find with me. Either way, the result won't be pretty, but for some reason, I can't disappoint him. I've thought about him all day, and I really want to see him tonight.

"Six-thirty," I reply.

"See you then, Evie." Panda, Evie, Love. The man is incapable of calling me by my name. I hate how much I like it.

There's a knock on my door at six-thirty sharp and I'm greeted by a smile that could make a nun tear off her clothes. He's dressed in loose jeans and a long sleeved button up. For half a second, I consider dragging his luscious ass to the bedroom, but I can't disappoint a kid.

"You look beautiful," he says, taking my hand after I usher him out, locking the door behind me.

"A vision in jeans," I reply, giving him a look. I really wish he'd quit with the bullshit lines. I'm not ugly, but I'm nowhere near beautiful. Before we can make it to the elevator, I find myself pinned against the hallway wall. His hand grips my hip as his other reaches to tilt my chin, forcing me to meet his gaze.

"I don't like being called a liar, Evie. You can be assured I mean every word I say," he whispers in my ear. "You're stunning. I can barely keep my hands off you." Warm sweet breath wafts across my neck. When he pulls back, his gaze falls to my lips, making me lick them. God, I want to feel his full lips on mine again. The corners of his mouth twitch in amusement. "Is there something you want, Evie?"

Ugh. Arrogant prick. If he thinks I'm asking him to kiss me, he's a few fries short of a Happy Meal. "To be on time." I'm relieved to hear my response come out smooth and strong, even though I feel like a trembling mess. It's ridiculous. He barely touched me. Just the thought of his kiss shattered my brain and set my heart racing.

"Have it your way, love." If I had it my way he'd be naked with my knees on his shoulders. He takes my hand as we wait for the elevator.

When the doors open, Ian grins at me and steps into the hall. "Ev, hey. I was just dropping by to say hi. I guess you're on your way out?" Oh, the lying little bastard. He just had to check out Mason.

Mason instantly drops my hand and slides his arm possessively around my shoulders. "You want to introduce me, sweetheart?" Sweetheart?!

"Uh...yeah, Mason, this is Ian, my uh...foster brother." Shit. Now I'm going to have to go through the whole 'grew up in foster care' story. "Ian, this is Mason."

"Her date," he clarifies. Great, is he going to piss on my leg?

"Nice to meet you," Ian replies, voice thick with amusement. We all step into the elevator and Mason keeps his arms around me, tucking me against his side. He smells fantastic.

"Don't you have a date tonight?" I ask Ian.

"Nah, but tomorrow I have two. Guess I'd better pick, huh?

I have to reschedule one. The blond is super hot with tits till Tuesday, but the redhead's more fun. What do you think, Ev?"

"I think you're a pig and you should cancel both of them."

His hand slides to cover his heart, his mouth falling open as he feigns offense. "I'm a perfect gentleman."

"I'm sure."

"Whew, nice car, man!" Ian exclaims as we step up to the curb.

A wide smile spreads across Mason's face. "I like it. What do you think, Evie?"

"It's pretty," I reply with a shrug, running my finger across the deep blue paint. This is the type of car I pictured him driving. "Where's your sedan?"

"At home." He grins.

Ian scoffs, shaking his head. "Pretty? Could you be any more of a girl right now? It's a Corvette. ZR1, right?"

"Yeah, 2013."

"Awesome."

"Okay, well, Ian, if you're done getting a hard on over Mason's car, we're going to go."

Ian flashes Mason a look of commiseration, mumbling, "Women."

Mason laughs. "Nice to meet you."

"You, too. Take care of her. She's one of the good ones." Ian winks at me while I glare back.

"So, do you think I passed the test?" Mason asks with a wink, pulling out into traffic.

"I think he was willing to sleep with you once he saw your car."

His tone turns serious. "Do I need to worry about him, Evie? He obviously cares for you."

He's jealous? We've been out once. "He's my friend. We've known each other since I was ten. I love him to death, but not like that. He doesn't want me that way, either. He pushed me to go out with you."

He cocks an eyebrow at me. "I'll be sure to thank him, although I'm not thrilled you needed convincing."

"Well, with your dumpy car and homely face, I'm sure you're used to it."

"It's a curse. I do my best to overcome." His grin fades a bit as he asks, "You met in foster care?"

"In a group home, yes."

"How long were you there?"

"In the system? Since I was five. In the home, from age ten until I aged out."

"I'm sorry."

"Don't be. I'm fine. It's a common story. Let's talk about something else. Like how I had no idea I'm dating a world champion fighter."

"It never came up."

"No wonder you looked at me like a nutcase when I asked if you fought professionally. You're famous."

"Not exactly." He laughs. "I'm not recognized that often. Only by the MMA fans."

I notice a small blue gift bag tucked between the seats. "What's this?"

"Plastic dinosaurs and green army men. I don't know what he's into, but for an eight year old, those are a safe bet." God, this guy is sweet. "What?" he asks, unnerved after I stare at him too long.

"If you're not careful, I might think you're a nice guy."

I'm rewarded with a wicked little smile. "I'll clear your mind of that notion later when I bend you over and make you scream."

"That sounds nice." His head falls back as his laughter fills the car.

The kids are gathered around the table when we arrive, just in time to see Matty blow out his candles. His eyes light up when we walk in. "Everly! Did you come to try our cake?"

"And to bring you a little present," I reply, handing him a small stuffed dog.

"Thanks, it has floppy ears," he exclaims with a grin.

"You're welcome. This is my friend, Mason. He wanted to come and wish you a happy birthday."

"Thanks," Matty repeats, staring up at Mason in awe. I can't blame the kid. I feel like a shrimp around him and I'm grown. "Dinos! Look, Danny!" A smile brightens his face as he displays his new toys. "And soldiers!"

"Awesome, buddy," Danny says, ruffling his hair.

After a piece of cake, I spend a few minutes chatting with Stacey, one of the girls counselors. "Good Lord, Ev, where'd you find that wet dream?" she exclaims.

"Shh! His head is big enough." I give a little nod at her sideways look. "Both of them." Mason glances up and smirks like he knows we're talking about him when we start laughing. He's sitting on his knees surrounded by a clutter of dinosaurs and army men, looking perfectly comfortable playing with Matty and the other two boys.

"I owe him a lasagna for dinner, so I guess we should go. Have you seen Danny? I wanted to see next week's schedule."

"He left before we cut the cake. Must've had a date." After the asshole guilted me into coming.

"I'll just check with him tomorrow."

The boys groan with disappointment when Mason announces we have to go. "Well, aren't you Mr. Popular," I tease as we return to his car.

He wraps his arm around my shoulders. "Aw, don't be jealous, love. No woman can play soldiers versus the zombie dinosaurs like I can."

"Zombie dinosaurs?"

"Created from the soldier's supersonic death rays, duh." He smiles at me. "I love your laugh, Evie. It's adorable."

His sincere compliment catches me off guard and I feel my cheeks flame. His smile widens and he runs his palm across my jaw. "I made you blush." I'm saved from my struggle to respond when his lips land on mine. The kiss is slow and soft and makes me want to climb into his seat and straddle him. When we break apart, he murmurs, "So sweet."

I don't know if he means me, my blush, or the kiss. Not that it matters since I seem to be incapable of speech again. He starts the car and moves us smoothly into the flow of traffic. "So, am I still invited to dinner?"

"And breakfast," I reply, squeezing his firm thigh.

"Only if you have Cocoa Pebbles."

"Park in the lot if you're staying the night," I advise as we approach my building. "My spots are in row C."

When he pulls in beside my Mini, I hear him curse. It takes a second for me to register my car is sitting on four flat tires and the windshield is shattered. "What the fuck!" I'm out of the seat and jerking open my driver's door before Mason can get the keys out of his ignition.

"Evie! Wait, damn it!"

"Someone trashed my car!" Anger streaks through me. Mason comes up beside me as I pick up a piece of paper from the seat. It's a note, written in bright red ink.

A little warning, bitch. Next time it'll be your face.

Cold fear trickles down my spine. Who would do this? I don't have any enemies.

"Evie." Mason's voice is calm. "What's the note say? Give it here."

I need to deal with this. He needs to go. This isn't his problem. "I'm sorry, but we need to cut our date short. I need to get a hold of my insurance company and..."

He huffs and snatches the paper from my hands. "I'm calling the police."

"No, it's probably some pissed off parent of one of the kids at BTC. They don't realize I'm not the one keeping them from their kid."

"It could also be some psycho husband from Striking Back. I don't give a shit who it is. They know where you live. You need to get inside." Mason pulls me to my feet and wraps his arm around me, keeping me tucked against him as he hurries us inside. "Are there cameras back here?"

"I have no idea. Slow down, you're overreacting."

"Just stay close to me."

As soon as we're safely in my apartment—and Mason has checked every room—he's on the phone to the cops. "They'll be here in the next hour," he tells me, obviously frustrated they didn't consider it an emergency.

"Okay, I may as well throw the lasagna in the oven. I'm starving." Two officers show up at my door nearly two hours later. They ask a few questions and fill out a report. Mason glares in their direction as they leave.

"Indy's finest," he growls. "They were a lot of help."

"Not much they can do. They dusted the car and the note for fingerprints. There are no cameras back there," I reply with a yawn.

"I have a security company that works with me. I'll put them on it in the morning. They can keep an eye on you, too. You need to be careful, Evie. Keep your phone on you, and don't go anywhere alone."

"Mason, it's sweet you're so worried about me, but really, you're overreacting. I don't need some bodyguard following me around."

"Fine, but I'm having them investigate."

"Uh-huh," I agree. I'm sleepy and it's easier than arguing.

His face softens. "Let's get you to bed. We'll talk about it in the morning."

Mason watches me with hooded eyes as I strip off my jeans and sweatshirt. Warm hands run up my sides before unclipping my bra and letting it fall to the floor. His lips are on my neck before I can take a breath. "So soft," he murmurs. "Such beautiful skin."

God, that voice. I turn around and seal my mouth to his, drinking in his taste as we remove his clothes. A growl rumbles through his chest when I squeeze his ass, and I'm scooped up and placed on the bed. I've never had a guy carry me to bed before him, and being swept up in those strong arms is a major turn on.

I lay on my back as he pulls off my lace panties and straddles my thighs, kneeling over me. "You have any clue what you do to me, Evie?" he asks, lust filled eyes sweeping over my body.

"I have a pretty good idea," I reply, my eyes on the rock hard proof bobbing over me. His eyes slam shut when I sit up and wrap my lips around him. I want to see this sexy confident man lose control. I want him at my mercy, and I get my wish. He's too big for me to take all of him, but I do my best. Judging by the unrestrained moans and the way air hisses through his clenched teeth, he's far from disappointed.

I love the way his hands cup my face, his fingers stroking lightly over my cheeks. Before he loses it completely, he pulls back and pushes me back onto the bed. His brow is furrowed as he quickly rolls on a condom, and my legs wrap around his hips, urging him on.

A wicked little half smile curls his lip when his fingers find me soaking wet. "So wet from sucking me," he teases, and I feel myself flush. I love and hate his dirty talk. No, I love it.

"Shut up and fuck me."

I barely get the words out before he obeys my order. Oh, does he obey it. It doesn't feel like fucking this time. Even when he's pounding into me, his eyes are on mine, and there's an undeniable connection. It relieves an ache, a loneliness I didn't even realize I had, and it scares the living shit out of me. I knew he was going to be trouble.

Chapter Five

A persistent buzzing wakes me early the next morning. Whoever is calling me this early is in deep shit. I snatch the vibrating phone from the nightstand and regard it with bleary eyes. I'm met with a picture of a smiling brunette and the words Selena calling. Who? Shit, this isn't my phone. It's Mason's.

Sitting up, I can hear water running. Mason's in the shower. After one more peek at the brunette's picture, I return his phone to the table. I really didn't mean to snoop. It's none of my business who she is. That's what I tell myself as I flop back into bed and pull the covers over my head.

I'm tempted to join Mason in the shower, but after last night, I'm pretty sore. I hear his deep chuckle before he crawls under the covers with me. "You really aren't a morning person, are you?"

"You've got me figured out," I reply, wrapping my arms around him.

"Can I lure you out with waffles? I know a great little café near here."

"I don't know. Last time I went there, I was followed by a stalker and his buddies."

"Brothers," he corrects.

"What?" I flip the blankets off of us.

"I was there with my brothers, Alex and Parker."

"It's unfair for one family to hoard that much hotness."

He growls and pins me to the bed. "I'm the hot one here. Don't you forget it." His stubble rasps against my neck and he nips my earlobe.

"Do you have any sisters?"

"No, all boys."

Damn it. So much for the brunette being his sister. His tongue traces my ear. "Mmm, okay, waffles it is. Let me get a quick shower," I say, hopping out of bed before I give in and attack him. "Do you have to get to work?"

"I have an intro class in a couple of hours. What are you doing today?"

"I'm at S.B. from one until four. No idea what they'll have me doing. The owner's a tyrant."

Laughing, he pulls me to my feet. "You should come to my gym this week."

"Is that a reference to my big ass?"

"Not that kind of gym, Panda. Today, I'm teaching grappling to middle schoolers, but Monday is a fight class with teens and adults."

"I'd love to come watch you get your ass kicked by adolescents. Oh, by the way, your phone was buzzing," I inform him, heading into the bathroom.

"Thanks, now hurry up before I take you again."

I flee the room before he can grab me. Good Lord, but this guy likes to mark me up. There's a tiny hickey on the side of my neck and another on my boob. For some reason, it makes me smile. I'm smiling at myself in the mirror like a moron when Mason rushes into the room. "Evie, I'm sorry, I have to go to work. I'll call you, okay?" He drops a quick kiss on my lips.

"Is everything all right?"

He seems flustered, although his eyes still take the time to flow over my nudity before he responds, "Everything's fine. Remember what you promised. Don't go anywhere alone, especially at night." He's out the door before I can reply.

Stunned, I stare after him for a moment. What the hell was that? He ran out like his hair was on fire and his ass was catching.

I continue to run scenarios through my mind as I shower. Was there a problem at Striking Back? He said he had to go to work. Did something happen at his gym? This is going to drive me crazy. The beep of an incoming text message from Amy interrupts my obsessing.

-Meet at Huddleston's?-

-Be there in thirty minutes.-

It's almost funny. I guess I get waffles after all.

Amy smiles as I slide into the booth across from her. "I'm going to assume I haven't heard from you because you're spending time with that god-like, tattoo covered man."

"And I'm going to assume the same about Wendy."

"Spill it, girl," she insists.

"I've spent a couple of nights with him." I grin as I recount my last week to my friend.

"A picnic, pandas, and hot monkey sex. Bitch, I hate you. You're making my life look boring. You'd better hang onto this one, Ev. He's something else." Her eyebrows raise as she glances at the door. "And speaking of, aren't those the hotties he was here with last time?"

I turn to see Mason's brothers settling at a corner table. "They're his brothers. Alex and Parker."

"Which is which?"

"No idea," I reply.

The waitress, Lacey, approaches us, smiling at our laughter. "You girls need to visit more often. You seem to bring the man meat with you."

"They come here a lot?" I ask.

"Not those two, but the one with the bright eyes was here just yesterday for breakfast. I'd set your sights on one of those two, though, sugar. Bright eyes usually comes in with a Latino chick."

The picture of Selena flashes before my eyes, and I quickly try to change the subject. "Looks like your new waitress is working out."

"So far so good. I hope I can keep her. You want your usual?"

"Yeah, thanks," I reply, glancing at Amy. Her face is pure sympathy. "It's okay," I assure her, after Lacey walks away. "We've only had a few dates. We haven't made any promises to each other."

"Ev, I've never seen you talk about a man the way you do him. It's not okay. Maybe she's a relative or friend."

That's seeming less and less likely. "He couldn't get out of my apartment fast enough when she called this morning." I explain his odd behavior.

Amy squeezes my hand. "Shit, Ev. Men are pigs."

"I'm aware."

"We need a night out. Sunday is race day. Let's go to the track Saturday night."

"You're on. Now, tell me how things are going with Wendy." Amy and I spend an hour catching up before I head to Striking Back.

I hate the dread I feel walking into a place I love. This is why I don't date those I work with. I've had fun with Mason. I mean, who wouldn't? He's gorgeous, sweet, funny, and fantastic in bed. He really seemed to be into me too, but it appears I'm one of many.

If he texts or finds me here, I'll let him know I can't see him anymore. I usually feel relieved when I make this decision, but for some reason I just feel heavy and tired. It's ridiculous. I'm in no mood to talk to anyone today. Fortunately, the kids and most of the parents are on a trip to the zoo. I spend a few hours doing laundry and helping prepare meals for the upcoming week. I can't help but glance at the cameras as I'm leaving.

Was he here today? Was he watching me on the monitors? Is he trying to figure out how to get rid of me, worrying I'll cause him trouble at work? He doesn't have to stress over that. I've never been the clingy type.

It's been seven days since I heard from Mason. I take that back. When I texted him on Wednesday with the message Hope everything's okay, I got back this winner, All fine. Busy with work. No talk of having me visit his gym. No flirty funny messages. It's clear he's done. I don't know why I even care. I'd already decided dating him was a bad idea.

What I need is a crazy night out with Amy, and tonight I'm going to get it. The night before the Indy 500 is a party like no other. Thousands of race fans and partiers from all over the country descend on the small neighborhood surrounding the track. The streets are closed to traffic and stuffed with people. Cops patrol, but only focus on the troublemakers. For one night, public intoxication and even public nudity is pretty much ignored. It's a blast.

Ian shows up at my door as I'm getting ready to go out. "Woo, look at you. Tight jeans and a tighter blouse. Where are you headed?"

"It's the night before the race!"

"You aren't going alone," he says with a frown.

"No, Dad, Amy is meeting me."

"Well, I'm coming too. Make sure some redneck doesn't pull you into an RV."

"Maybe I want to be ravaged in an RV." I laugh, locking my door before we head to the elevator.

He glances at me after I buckle myself in his car. "You get your car back?"

"Yep. Good as new."

"Still no idea who did that shit?"

"No, some prank probably."

After a few seconds of silence, he asks, "Still haven't heard from Mason?"

"We're done."

"Who decided?"

I gaze out the window, watching the city go by as I answer, "Since he never contacted me so I could tell him I'm done, I guess he gets credit for this one."

"The guy's a moron to break up with you, pup." Ian reaches

to squeeze my hand.

"We weren't together, so it wasn't really a breakup." I look around with a smile as Ian pays a guy twenty bucks to park on his lawn. "Besides, I'm ass deep in horny men at the moment. I don't give a shit about Mason."

It's far from the truth. I let him get under my skin, and I can't seem to shake him. My usual response would be to find a cute guy to bang my brains out, someone who won't care if I leave right after. For some reason, it just isn't appealing this time. I'm just going to get drunk and have fun with my friends.

We make our way through the boisterous drunken crowd to meet Amy on the corner of Sixteenth and Georgetown. She has her arm around her girlfriend, Wendy, and they wave, excited to see us. "Hey, Wendy, I'm glad you made it," I say, giving Amy a quick hug.

"If I get fired for calling in to work sick, I'm blaming Amy." She laughs. "She's a bad influence."

"So, where are we going, ladies?" Ian drapes his arm around me.

"The Blue Stripe? I need a drink," I reply.

"You heard the woman." Wendy laughs, and we head down the street. The best thing about the night before the race is the diversity of the people. They come from all over the country. I've even met people from Australia and England here. And everyone is trashed and happy.

Ian elbows me. "Ev, look, they caught one." We all watch with wide smiles while a young guy chases a twenty dollar bill blowing down the road. The crowd parts, letting him through. Just as his fingers almost touch the edge of the bill, it scoots a few more feet. The guy is so focused on getting the money before someone else sees it, he doesn't realize he's being watched by a crowd of people.

When he reaches for the bill a third time and it moves again, he looks up and realizes he's been tricked. His cheeks redden and he drops his forehead into his hands as the crowd bursts into laughter. The man standing on the curb holding a fishing pole and reeling in the twenty dollar bill waves at him, and the young guy flips him off before starting toward him.

I watch as the man tosses him a beer and slaps him on the back. The young guy's buddies join the man and his friends as they set up the bait for the next sucker. "That never gets old." I laugh.

We're crossing the parking lot of The Blue Stripe when a thick stream of water douses a woman in front me, turning her shirt nearly transparent. "Asshole!" she screeches, before stalking toward the bar. A line of incredibly hot men are laughing and elbowing each other while she stomps away. Unfortunately, they notice us.

"Ow! That's what I'm talkin' 'bout." A stocky blond guy gestures toward their sign that reads Show us your tits. "Let's see them, ladies."

Amy laughs and shakes her head until I point out the man with the water cannon. Where the hell did he get that thing? It's a huge syringe, minus the needle, that must hold at least a gallon of water. He submerges it in a cooler and pulls back the plunger, a wicked smile on his face. Okay, so it's flash them or get soaked.

"Come on," I yell, smiling. "You don't want to see mine. They're little!"

"I want to lick'em baby, but I'll settle for a peek."

"Hey," Ian yells. "I could be her boyfriend."

"It's okay," his buddy replies. "He ain't the jealous type." Everyone laughs, and I catch them off guard by jerking my shirt and bra up, giving the guys a look. Hey, this party only happens once a year.

"Beautiful, baby," the blond calls.

The man with the water cannon points at Amy and Wendy. "Next!"

"Just so you know, you're ogling lesbian boobs," Amy teases as she and Wendy raise their shirts. The crowd laughs when Ian stands between them and flashes his chest, squeezing a nipple for good measure.

The men are still yelling when we head away from them. "Did you see the blond? I'd drink her bathwater. I bet I can run faster horny than she can scared." The comments and laughter fade when we make our way into the bar. Ian finds us a table in the back, and the shots commence. I'm lit up like Times Square when my phone beeps with a text from Mason.

-Evie, just got back in town. Can we talk?-

"Is that him?" Amy demands, noting the look on my face. I nod and stare at the phone, debating whether to reply when it vibrates in my hands. Amy snatches it. "Oh, no, you're having fun. Don't let him fuck you up."

She's right. He ran out after some other chick and ignored me for a week. "Keep it," I reply, as it buzzes again.

"I'll do better than that, hun." Before I can stop her, she accepts the call. "Everly's phone." Her smile is gleeful as she says, "Oh, hello, Jason. Sorry, Ev's on the dance floor shaking her ass. You'll have to call back."

I can't hear Mason's reply, but it doesn't sound cheerful. "She has guys lined up to dance with her, don't think she needs another tonight. I'll tell her you called, Jason."

"Mason!" I hear him shout. He's still talking when she ends the call and mutes the phone.

"Let him stew on that a bit." Everyone should have a friend like Amy. "Listen, Ev, I have to tell you something. I'm sort of...moving to New York City with Wendy."

I nearly choke on my drink. "You're what? When?"

"Next week." She looks up with a guilty expression. "I just found out a few days ago. Wendy got her dream job, and since my company has an office there as well, they agreed to transfer me."

I don't know what to say. Amy has been a close friend for years. "Are you sure this is what you want to do?" She nods, and I lean to give her a hug. "I'm coming to visit you constantly, you bitch."

"You better. We'll be dorky tourists together. Now, no more sad talk, let's dance." Nearly two hours later, I'm soaked in sweat and exhausted from dancing. I'm also regretting all those shots. I can't remember ever being so drunk. Of course, at the moment, I can't remember my own phone number, so it's not surprising.

Amy and Wendy are getting freaky on the dance floor, and

Ian is sitting across the room with a giggling girl in his lap. I should go, but I'll never get a cab on race night. I check my phone and find three text messages from Mason. I'm not reading them. It's bad enough I'm still thinking about him. The guy at the door even looks like him. Shit on toast, it is him. How did he find me? It doesn't matter because I'm not talking to him.

The room spins when I stand and make a beeline for the dance floor, trying to blend in with the crowd. I'm instantly sandwiched between two guys, dancing against me. Mason's eyes meet mine, and I reach back to put my arms around the guy's neck behind me, deliberately pushing my breasts into the man grinding against my hips.

I can almost hear Mason's growl as he pushes between us. "Come on, Evie. You're drunk and I'm taking you home."

"Oh, is it my turn again? Fuck off, Mason," I slur.

"I just want to get you home safe."

"You just want to fuck me. Well, maybe I don't want you, Mr. Arrogant. Maybe I want to fuck...him," I announce, grabbing a random guy. The guy smiles as I grab his hips. "You won't run away when some chick calls you and then ignore me for a week, will you?"

"No way, baby. My name's Brad."

Mason is seething. "Everly, you're coming with me. Don't make me beat this guy's ass." Mason grips my waist, pulling me toward him. When Brad gets a good look at Mason, his eyes widen.

"You're Mason Reed! I watched you fight The Intimidator a few years ago. You were awesome!" He steps away from me. "Sorry, I didn't know she was your girl."

"I'm not his..." My protest is interrupted when the room tilts. All I can see is the floor and tons of feet, but I can hear the laughter as he carries me back to my table over his shoulder. "Put me down! Are you insane?" He ignores my fists pounding his back.

"I'm getting there, lady. Now, sit and drink some water, then, I'm taking you home."

Ian, Amy and Wendy return to the table, eyeing us cautiously. "Want to introduce us?"

"Sure, Amy, Wendy, meet the cave man who suddenly thinks he owns me."

Mason flashes a heart stopping smile at my friends. "I'm Mason. It's nice to meet you."

"Where you been, Mason?" Amy demands.

"I had an emergency to take care of. When Evie is sober enough to remember, I'll explain. For now, I'm taking her home. I'm happy to give you guys a ride if you'd like."

"Thanks," Ian replies. "I don't see making it back to my car tonight."

It's the middle of the night, but the crowd outside hasn't thinned. It usually doesn't until dawn. The cool night air sobers me a bit, and I laugh at the sight of the same men still loitering at the far end of the parking lot. They've retired the water cannon and have apparently settled for fucking with people as they walk by. "I know those boobs!" the blond calls with a drunken smile, gesturing to me, Amy and Wendy.

"We're hard to forget," Amy calls.

The dark headed one points at me. "Hey, beautiful, can we get one more peek?"

Mason's arm tightens around my waist, and I consider flashing them again just to show him he can't control me. And to piss him off, because even though I know we weren't really dating, his disappearance hurt me. "She's mine, asshole," Mason says, not unkindly. He's trying to make light of it, go along with the party atmosphere. I'm sure he spent time out here with a Free Breast Exam sign of his own.

"Just because there's a goalie doesn't mean I can't score," the guy calls back, his buddy slapping him on the back.

I feel Mason tense, and Ian looks prepared to intervene. Damn it. "Sorry, my goalie's stick is bigger than yours," I shout, slurring a bit. The crowd laughs along with the guys. Crises averted.

"Did you really show them your tits?" Mason asks.

"Don't see why you'd care," I reply.

"They liked the way she shook them," Amy adds, stirring up shit in the best way.

Mason shakes his head, but doesn't comment.

"Where did you park?" I grumble as we turn another corner. I'm not sure how much longer I can stay on my feet.

"We're almost there."

"We really appreciate the ride," Wendy tells Mason, and Ian and Amy agree. Ugh, I'm going to smack them all just as soon as I can see them again. Shit's getting blurry. I barely remember climbing into Mason's back seat with Amy and Wendy, trying to separate from him. He must've dropped them off first, because at some point I realize they're gone, and Ian and Mason are talking in low voices.

"If you aren't into her, man, then leave her alone. She's had enough shit from guys."

"I am into Evie. Fuck, I've been thinking about her all week." Really couldn't tell on my end.

"Then don't give up. She gives a new meaning to the word stubborn." Ian chuckles, climbing out of the car. Traitor.

"Any other advice?"

"Yeah, if she remembers you carrying her off the dance floor, guard your balls." They laugh before Ian shuts the door. I need to remember to kick him in the balls.

My head spins and the next thing I know sunlight is streaming through my bedroom window, and someone has planted a hatchet in my head. I wince at the sound of the front door slamming. God, why did I drink so much? "Ian?" I call, my voice hoarse.

Instead of Ian, Mason's grinning face appears in my doorway. How did he get in? "What the hell are you doing here?" I ask, closing my eyes and trying to quiet the thump thumping of my brain.

Doubt flashes across his face before he shakes his head. "Do you remember last night at all?"

I have to think about it. Mason showed up at the bar and acted all Neanderthal. I flashed some guys. He dropped off my friends. Damn, it appears my memory ends in his car. Did I fuck him? I jerk back the covers to see I'm wearing a t-shirt and panties, and not the ones I left the house in.

"Nothing happened, Evie. You had alcohol spilled on your clothes. I helped you get a shower and put you to bed. That's all. I slept on the couch." While I'm grateful he didn't take advantage, I can't help but see it as evidence he isn't interested in sex with me anymore. So why is he here?

"What are you doing here?" I repeat, forcing myself upright, groaning when my head protests.

"I brought you home. You were trashed, and I didn't want to leave you alone."

"That was nice of you. I'm fine now. You can go."

Ignoring my petulant comment, he leaves the room and returns with a glass of orange juice and two ibuprofen. "Take these. You'll feel better. Do you think you can eat some toast?"

Food is the last thing I want. "No thanks. I appreciate the ride home and all, Mason, but I just want to sleep off this hangover. I'll call you later," I lie.

He frowns and sits on the edge of the bed. "Evie, I'm sorry I didn't call."

"Stop," I interrupt, holding up my palm. "You don't owe me an explanation. I'm not your girlfriend."

"I know, but we had a lot of fun together and I really like you. I want to spend more time with you, and I hope you want that too."

I lean back against the headboard, keeping the covers pulled to my waist. "A week with me, then a week with her? Sorry, just because I'm not looking for a relationship doesn't mean I'm cool with sending you off to fuck someone else when we aren't together." His brow furrows as I continue. "I like you too, and I did have fun, but I think it's time to give it a rest." Before you tear my heart out and stomp on it. I have no doubt he can. I've really missed him this week, drove myself half crazy wondering why he didn't call, and that's just not me. I'm the one who doesn't call. I'm the one who moves on.

"I'm not fucking anyone else. Why would you think that?" His gaze is intense.

"I'm sure Selena would be heartbroken you've forgotten her so quickly."

He looks at me like I've just escaped the nuthouse. "You think I'm fucking Selena?"

"Everything was fine until she called, then you couldn't get away from me fast enough. Your quick escape was followed by a vanishing act. It's not hard to figure out."

He sighs and runs his hands through his hair. "Selena works for me, that's all. She's married, and I'm certainly not fucking her. I wasn't lying when I said I had to work. It was a last minute emergency that took me out of the country for a week."

"What kind of emergency?"

He moves to sit beside me. "My job is complicated and sometimes shit happens at the last second that I have to deal with."

Could he be more vague? "Outside the U.S.?"

"Striking Back helps build and fund abuse shelters in a few other countries. I don't get called away for that long very often, but it happens. Usually, Alex or Parker handle the overseas management."

"Oh." It's all I can say. I've been a jealous wreck and I feel foolish and embarrassed.

He takes my hand, entwining our fingers. "I wasn't with anyone else."

"I'm sorry. I don't have the right to tell you who you can see when we aren't exclusive."

He grins and wraps his arm around me, tucking me against his side. "I'm glad you missed me, and I'm not opposed to exclusivity. I want you to myself."

"I didn't say I missed you," I point out, stalling as his offer sinks in. I think I just argued myself into a relationship I'm completely unprepared for.

"Well, I missed you. Go away with me."

"Excuse me?"

"I'll take a few days off work, and we'll go somewhere. I want to spend some time with my girlfriend."

Girlfriend. Do I want to be his girlfriend? He's too good to be true, too good to last. I'm already crazy about him. Can I really deal with another heartbreak when he leaves? He isn't giving me time to think. It shouldn't be a hard decision, should it? Stay home and stick to my same boring routine, or run away with a tattoo covered God and fuck our brains out. No decision really.

I know spending more time with this man I'm already too attached to isn't a smart choice. Unfortunately, my brain doesn't seem to be all that active in the decision making process. I want to be with him. "Camping?" I suggest, after a few moments of silence.

A wide smile appears and he chuckles, "You're perfect."

"Yeah, don't forget it again."

"Why don't we leave in the morning? I know you don't feel well."

"Okay," I agree, stretching back out on the bed. Call me when you wake up tomorrow?"

He huffs and gets to his feet. "Quit trying to get rid of me, Evie. It's not happening. I'm going to hang out today and take care of you."

"You are, huh?"

"Yep, Deal with it. I'm not giving you a chance to change your mind."

"You think because you have a big cock, I'm going to give you your way all the time?" I tease.

"No, that'll be because I know how to use it to make you scream. Now, I'm going to get us some takeout and movies." He leaves the room and returns with a bottle of water. "Drink this, and take a nap."

"Again with the orders."

"Fine. Please drink the water and take a nap."

"Was that so hard?"

"It's always hard when I'm near you. Feel better, Panda. I really want to fuck you in a tent." He kisses me on the forehead and leaves the room before I can think of a reply. Really, what do you say to that?

A call from Ian wakes me a few hours later. "Hung over?" he asks, and I know he's grinning.

"Not so bad now. How about you?"

"I'm never hung over. So, did you work things out with

Mason, or do I need to kick his ass?"

"Apparently, I have a boyfriend."

"Whoa. That's great, Ev. It's about damn time."

"Shut up. I don't know how I feel about it yet." I drop my voice, unsure if Mason is nearby.

"You're scared. Get over it and give the guy a chance."

"I am."

"A real chance. Quit looking for any little reason to tell yourself it won't work."

"I don't do that!"

"You left the last guy after the second date because he cracked his knuckles."

"Well, yeah, it was annoying."

"Ev," he sighs.

"I'll give him a chance. He's…different."

"And you're crazy about him."

"Yes," I admit. "We're going away for a couple of days. Camping, so you probably won't hear from me."

"Have fun and call me when you get back."

"I will. Love ya."

"Love ya."

Mason walks in as I end the call, a brilliant smile on his handsome face. "I picked up movies and pizza. You going to get your ass out of bed?" We spend the day snuggled on the couch, watching movies. When we move to the bedroom, he only cuddles me close and kisses me goodnight. "Get some sleep, baby. We have an early day."

That's an understatement. We're up before the sun, packing and getting ready. Strong arms envelop me from behind and I shiver at the warmth of his breath in my ear. "You have to stop flaunting that plump little ass in front of me, or we won't make it to the woods." He slaps my ass, making me jump.

"I can't believe you've never been to Turkey Run. Trail three is amazing," I exclaim, turning my head to kiss him. "I'll try not to wear you out, old man."

"Wear me out? I'm going to fuck you until every animal in the forest knows my name."

"What the hell are we waiting for?" I grab my backpack, and he laughs, following me to his car.

"We have one stop to make first," he announces with a sheepish smile. "I promised to meet my brothers for breakfast today. Do you mind?"

He wants to introduce me to his family? "Breakfast with three hot men? I'll suffer through it."

"One hot man and two unfortunate looking younger brothers," he corrects, pulling into a parking space at a small restaurant. His brothers are seated at a table on the patio.

"Everly, this is Alex and Parker." He glares at his siblings. "Be nice, assholes."

Alex smiles, showing perfectly straight white teeth. He's the polar opposite of Mason with curly blond hair and light brown eyes. "It's nice to meet you, Everly. Mason never shuts up about you."

"It's interminable," Parker adds. "Evie this and Evie that. I can see why, though. You're gorgeous. Come, sit next to me."

"Don't make me kick your ass," Mason growls, pulling out my chair.

"You could try, but I'd hate to embarrass you in front of your girl." Parker winks at me. He has Mason's dark hair, cut much shorter, and his pale blue eyes twinkle as he baits his brother.

"Ignore them, Everly," Alex advises, handing me a menu. "Everything's a competition with them."

"Thanks. Do you want to order, Mason? I mean, if your biggest pecker contest is over."

"No contest there, baby," he replies, kissing my cheek.

"Dude, I'll whip it out right now," Parker threatens.

"Behave," Alex says with a long suffering sigh. The way they insult each other, play off one another, is hilarious. Under all the name calling is a clear bond of love and affection. Family. They're eager to answer any questions about Mason, especially if they can embarrass him with the answer.

"So, are you both single?" I ask, after watching Parker flirt with the waitress.

"Why, baby? You interested?" Parker replies, earning a

smack in the back of the head from Mason.

"I'm seeing a guy," Alex replies. "It's too early to introduce him to these idiots though. Don't want to send him running."

That explains Alex's lack of interest in the cute waitress. "I completely understand." I laugh. Mason and Parker fake identical wounded expressions.

"Your girl just insulted us," Parker says.

"Yeah, I like her," Alex tells Mason with a grin.

Mason puts his arm around me. "She's one of a kind."

Chapter Six

We're happy and upbeat during the hour and a half drive to Turkey Run State Park. "Your brothers are funny."

He smiles at me. "They're okay."

"You're obviously close."

"We are. They're my pain in the ass kid brothers, but we'd do anything for each other." He cocks his eyebrow and gazes at me. "They sure liked you."

"Well, of course."

He laughs. "I'm glad you decided to come. Did I pull you away from anything important?"

"I called a friend to take my hours at Building Tomorrow's Child, and the owner of Striking Back assured me they have everything covered."

"How many days a week do you volunteer?"

"Four or five, depends on when I'm needed. There's a literacy program starting in the fall I plan to participate in."

"So, you don't have a job?"

"No."

"How do you...shit, this is probably none of my business, but how do you make your money?"

I was wondering when that would come up and his nervous expression makes me laugh. "I sell a little Meth here and there."

"Very funny, baby."

"I inherited it."

He frowns, confused. "I thought you didn't have any family."

"I don't, but apparently my parents were loaded when they died. I was lucky. When I aged out of the system at eighteen, I had enough money for ten lifetimes. A lot of foster kids end up on the street or in prison. I don't have to work. The least I can do is help."

"You're amazing, do you know that?" he asks, taking my hand as we turn into the park.

"I'm not the one who built a domestic violence shelter."

He smiles at me before turning to pay the park attendant. "Let's find a campsite."

We follow the narrow paved road as it winds through the woods, dotted on either side by worn dirt campsites. It's not quite summer yet so most of them are empty, and we choose a spot right across from the showers.

Mason puts up the tent while I make a neat pile of firewood. We want to get everything ready for the night before we get into any activities. Leaning against a tree, I watch him pound in the stakes holding the guy wires.

He's shirtless and a light sheen of sweat coats his chest. His eyes seem to glow in the afternoon sunlight. The flex and pull of muscles in his back mesmerizes me, and he's gazing at me with a grin when I realize he's calling my name. Probably has a couple of times.

"I'm feeling a little exposed. You're totally objectifying me. It's just wrong, Evie." Ugh, the smirk on his face.

My cheeks heat and there's no playing it off this time. This calls for alternate measures. I approach him and slide my hand up his chest. "You don't like me looking at you?" His lips part and I feel his heartbeat increase under my palm. I love that I can affect him this way.

"When you look at me like that, I have to fight the urge to strip you naked right here."

"That's not exactly a deterrent," I reply, and he chuckles.

"Tonight, baby. I'm going to lick every inch of this delicious body." He runs his hands down my back, resting them on my ass.

Hot lips land on my neck, raising goose bumps on my skin.

"Promise?" I whisper.

"Oh, yes, love." He takes my lips with his in a slow kiss. "I promise. Now, what should we do first?"

I step back, putting a little space between us. "We could go hiking, or there's a two hour canoe trip that starts at three."

"Have you ever been in a canoe?"

"Nope, you?"

"No, let's do it." He locks the cooler in the car and grabs his bag. "I have plenty of supplies in here if things go all Deliverance on us."

"I'm not worried. You're the one with the pretty mouth." I laugh, and he takes my hand as we start toward the river.

The guy in charge of the canoes looks about fourteen years old. He hands us both a life jacket, and Mason asks, "This isn't a guided trip?"

"No, sir. Just follow the river. There's a wide bank with a sign that'll tell you where the trip ends. A van will bring you back here. The water is only about four feet deep except for a few areas, mainly under the bridges and rock outcroppings. Keep your life jackets on."

We thank him and head down to pull our canoe into the water. It's very still and calm, and it's a good thing. We need some practice. "We're going sideways!" I squeal, and Mason laughs.

"Put your oar on the left side."

I do and we straighten out. "I'm no good at this," I announce, laughing.

"You're doing great, baby. Having fun?"

"This is awesome." We float along peacefully, and I take the opportunity to drink in my surroundings. The scent of trees, wet leaves and honeysuckle fills my nostrils and I close my eyes, breathing it in.

I'm immersed in the tranquility of the forest. The wind rattling the leaves, the buzz of the dragonflies hovering a few feet above our heads, the water lapping against the boat. It's such a reprieve from the usual sounds of traffic, airplanes and chattering people. When I open my eyes, Mason is staring at me.

"What?"

"You look beautiful out here. So happy."

"I am. This is how people were meant to live. Free, natural, not packed together in concrete rows."

"Why don't you move to the country?" he asks softly.

"I've thought about it, but I don't want to leave Ian and Amy. Although, Amy will be leaving for New York soon. Still, BTC needs me, and I really enjoy working at Striking Back."

"You're very popular with the residents and staff, you know," he informs me.

"The women are so brave, and the resilience of the kids is inspiring."

He gestures to a sign informing us we're at the halfway point. "Want to stop for a few and stretch our legs?"

"Sure." We drag the canoe onto the bank and sit at the edge with our feet in the water. Mason digs into his backpack and produces a tube of sunscreen. "Mr. Prepared," I murmur, and he smiles at me.

"You're getting red." He rubs the cool lotion on my shoulders and the back of my neck. "Close your eyes, love." I feel the pads of his fingers as he gently massages the lotion into my cheeks, nose, and forehead. "Can I ask you something, Everly?" His voice is soft. I'm pretty sure I won't like the question.

"Mmm Hmm."

Strong hands massage my shoulders. "How did you end up in foster care? What happened to your parents?"

I suppose it was bound to come up. "There was a car accident when I was five. I was the only survivor."

"I'm sorry." He pulls me back against his chest and kisses my neck.

"Don't be. It was a long time ago. Are your parents still alive?"

His chest rises on a deep sigh. "My mom died when I was ten. I was raised by my aunt and uncle."

"Your brothers too?"

"Yeah, we were lucky to have Aunt Linda and Uncle Logan."

"What about your dad?"

Relief floods his features when we're interrupted by shrieks and laughter as a group of four canoes filled with teenagers come into view, saving him from answering. They paddle to the shore with the same idea as us, a break at the halfway point. "Thank God!" One of the girls cries, darting into the woods. "I really gotta pee!" The others laugh at her and plop down on the bank. So much for our peace and quiet.

"Let's go, love," Mason says, pulling me to my feet. The last hour of our canoe ride is peaceful and soothing. I can't help but think how close Mason came to growing up like I did. He lost his parents as a child too. What a thing to have in common. I'm sorry for him, but I also feel closer to him. I wonder how his mother died, and what happened to his father, but I don't want to push.

As we float around the last bend in the river, we enter some rapids and our speed increases quickly. "Woo!" I yell, loving the thrill of it, the wind through my hair.

Mason laughs. "Hold it steady, Evie." We're fine until the right side of the canoe catches on a large underwater boulder. The next thing I know I'm submerged in the freezing water. A split second later, I'm floating in the calm pool at the foot of the rapids, and Mason's swimming toward me.

"You okay?"

"That was amazing!" I cry, and he snorts. When he puts his hands on my shoulders, panic grips me. "Don't push me under!"

He stares at me like I've lost my mind. "I wasn't going to."

"Shit. Sorry, I...can't stand being dunked. I didn't mean to freak out."

"It's okay. I'm sorry I scared you." He points to our canoe, now upside down and beached on a shallow area. "I can see the return area. Let's get going so we can get dried off."

"Sounds good."

The boy collecting the canoes laughs as we drag it ashore. "I saw you go over. You'd be surprised how many people make it all the way, then flip right there. Come on, I'll drive you back before you freeze to death." He drops us at our campsite, and we gather our clothes and race for the showers, giggling like kids.

"Hang on," Mason says, and enters the men's side. Finding it empty, he grabs my hand and tugs me inside, locking the door. Two grimy stone shower stalls stand side by side.

"I'm so not fucking in here."

"I just don't want you in the women's side alone. Some creep could come in." Mason adjusts the water and gestures for me to go first. "I'll use the next one."

The hot water feels amazing. Mason is washed and dressed by the time I finish rinsing my hair. "Sorry." I hurry to dress when we hear a knock at the door.

"One second," Mason calls. I yank my sweatshirt over my head and nod at him to unlock the door. We're met by two smirking men, obviously amused to find us there. "All yours, guys," Mason says as I stare at the ground and make a quick exit. Mason catches up with me. "Aw, you're embarrassed."

"You know what they think." I slap him.

"Good. Everyone should know you're mine."

"Neanderthal."

"You better believe it, baby. You hungry?"

"Starving." My stomach chooses that moment to growl, and Mason chuckles.

"I'll make dinner." Mason removes the cooler from the car while I build a fire. He pulls out a few wrapped packages and proceeds to slide chunks of beef, peppers, and red potatoes onto metal skewers before laying them on a rack over the fire.

"Anything I can do?"

"There's a bottle of wine in the cooler."

"You thought of everything," I tease. After the kabobs have cooled, we sit by the fire to eat. "This is delicious," I exclaim.

"Thank you." A shy smile graces his lips. God, he can go from sexy to adorable in less than a second.

"I've had a great time with you today."

"Me too, Panda. Although, you scared the shit out of me when we tipped that canoe. I couldn't find you for a second."

"Don't worry, I can swim."

He reaches to slide a chunk of green pepper between my lips. "Do you want to tell me why you thought I was going to push you under?"

"It's not that I thought you would. I just...panicked." His eyes are a deep blue in the firelight as they stare into mine, and I suddenly find my feet interesting. "I don't really remember much of the car accident that killed my parents, but I remember the water. We drove off a bridge into a lake, and I was trapped underwater. I remember the cold and the dark, the water pressing in. Then I woke in a hospital."

A rough hand grips mine, pulling me down into his arms, onto a double sleeping bag he's laid by the fire. "I understand, love." And I think he does. Most people think they get it, that they know how you feel, but that's bullshit. But Mason has known grief, and I suspect there's more to his story that I've yet to find out. He seems to be a happy man, but there's an undercurrent of melancholy that shines in his eyes when he's quiet. As if he's reaching for something he can't quite grasp.

He pulls a blanket over us, bringing his lips to mine, and I decide now isn't the time to question him. "Do you want to go to the tent?"

"Later," he murmurs. "I want to love on you under the stars." I gaze up through the treetops at the sky bursting with glittering beauty. "I'm going to drive you crazy." Soft hair tickles my belly as he drops kisses from my navel to my breasts, his forehead forcing my sweatshirt up beneath my arms.

My nipples tighten in the cool night air. "Someone could see us," I whisper as he slides my shirt the rest of the way off.

"This place is nearly deserted. It's just us, baby." The sensation of his mouth on my nipple steals any further argument. After my other breast is blessed with the same treatment, he brings his hot mouth to mine, kissing me like I hold the only oxygen in the world.

I unfasten his jeans and shove them down where he can kick them off, along with his boxer briefs. He returns the favor, then pulls off his shirt, leaving us both naked by the fire, only a thin blanket hiding us from any prying eyes. I love how he groans when I lick across his nipple. "Evie." Sliding down my body, he licks and kisses until his tongue slips between my legs. Oh shit. I throw my head back, staring at the stars as he devours me. So intense. So beautiful. I have to have him. Here. Now.

"Mason." I pull him up by his hair and grab his cock. He's a monster, solid as steel and pulsing in my palm. "Tell me you have condoms."

With a deep chuckle, he reaches into his jean pocket and produces one, wasting no time rolling it on. "You sure you want this out here?"

"Don't talk me out of it now."

"Wouldn't think of it."

I can't help but cry out when he sinks completely into me, stretching me past my limit. "You're so big," I groan.

"You're so tight. So fucking good." I wrap my legs around him as he arches above me, fucking me—no—he's making love to me. His eyes never leave mine as he takes me higher and higher until we both lose control, filling the forest with our groans of satisfaction and ecstasy.

He buries his face in my neck while he catches his breath. "You're amazing, Everly."

"Funny, I was just thinking the same about you."

"Are you cold? Do you want to move to the tent?"

"Mmm, you're warm. I just want to lie here a minute." He flops onto his back and I cuddle up to him, resting my cheek on his chest.

It feels so good, lying here with him. The stars shine above us and the fire casts a soft glow around us, pushing back the dark. I can't remember a time I've felt more relaxed and content.

"Evie, baby, wake up." Where the hell am I? The sky is barely light when Mason kisses my jaw. "As much as I hate to cover up that sweet body, you need to get dressed."

Shit. We slept outside all night. Naked. At some point, Mason covered us with a sleeping bag in addition to the blanket.

My hair is damp with morning dew, but wrapped in Mason's arms, I don't feel cold. I'm greeted with a soft smile. "Good morning, love."

"Morning. Why didn't you wake me to move to the tent?"

"You looked comfortable."

"Mmm, I am, but I don't want to flash people when they come to shower."

"Keep the blanket wrapped around you and dress in the tent." I nearly drool over the sight of his bare ass as he rises and walks to unzip the tent without a hint of concern. His laughter echoes through the forest while I try to retrieve my jaw from the ground. "You coming? It's a little chilly."

"You have no shame." I giggle, slapping his ass before ducking inside. Once we're dressed, we head toward The Inn Restaurant for breakfast. "We're really roughing it," I tease as a waitress brings our food.

"I need some sustenance after last night."

"You'll need it more for our hike today." I spread the map out in front of him. "It's marked 'very rugged'."

"As long as you don't wuss out and make me piggyback you once you're tired."

"I hiked this trail when I was seven," I scoff.

"Let's do it." He drops a few bills on the table and takes my hand. This man has held my hand more in the last two days than anyone else has in my life.

We return to the tent to grab some supplies for the hike and we're off. Trail three is a beautiful hike, and I'm thrilled to show Mason. None of the men I've dated before would have given two shits about seeing the amazing rock formations and winding hollows, but he seems as enamored as I am.

"Wow," he breathes as we crest a hill and find ourselves on a large rock outcrop. It overlooks the river and miles of forest surrounding it. Stepping up behind me, he slips his arms around my waist and pulls me back against his chest.

"Gorgeous, isn't it? I'd love to see it in winter, covered in snow."

"It's a date," he says, resting his chin on my shoulder.

"You and your long term dates. You love to plan ahead, don't you?" I press a kiss on his lips, secretly thrilled he thinks we'll still be dating by then.

"Nothing wrong with long term, love." His words pierce something inside me. No matter how I fight to avoid relationships, long term love is all I've ever wanted.

After gazing at the scenery for a few minutes, we're joined by more hikers. Shit. It's the two men who caught us using the men's shower. Their hands are clasped, and the one with curly hair grins at us.

"Hey guys," Mason greets. "Would you mind taking our picture?"

"Sure," the other man answers, taking Mason's phone. After he takes a photo, he asks us to do the same for them. They put their arms around each other, and I snap the photo.

"They were adorable," I remark as we move on.

Mason laughs. "You're adorable."

I peek up at him. "So, your brother Alex is gay?"

"Picked up on that, did you?" He grins down at me.

"Do you get along well?"

"With Alex? Sure. It's Parker that bears watching. You saw how he flirted with you."

"I'm sure he was only teasing."

"Only because you're with me. Otherwise, he'd be all over you."

"You don't know that!" I shove him playfully.

"He's my brother and I love him, but he's the biggest whore in Indy."

"Ian could probably give him some competition." I laugh.

We're both pleasantly tired and sore when we return to our campsite. Mason makes a delicious pot of chili over the fire. "Oh my god, this is fantastic," I moan, taking my last bite.

Before Mason can respond, there's a crack of thunder and the skies open up. Laughing, I throw our backpacks in the tent and we dive in after. Mason gives me a wicked grin, quickly stripping off my clothes. Fuck. I get to make love to Mason in a tent during a thunderstorm. Life is good. The storm pounds the tent for hours, but Mason has no problem keeping up.

Chapter Seven

My head is still in the clouds when I arrive at my apartment. I just want to soak in a hot bath and reminisce about my perfect trip with Mason. First, I need to call Ian. "Hey girl, I was beginning to wonder about you. Thought he might have you tied to a tree somewhere. How did it go?"

I can't help the smile on my face, remembering his body arched above me in the moonlight. "It was fun." I grab my mail and switch the phone to speaker so I can open a thick manila envelope.

"Just fun?"

"We hiked, swam, and went canoeing. Talked a lot."

"That sounds like a good sign."

"Oh fuck! No! Goddamn it!" I shout as a pile of photos slide out of the envelope.

"Ev? What's wrong?" Ian asks, but I barely hear him.

In the first photo, Mason sits with his arm around a thin blonde woman. Her head is bent, and their hands are clasped. Another shows him embracing a petite red headed woman, his hand resting on her back. I don't want to see the rest. "I have to go. Talk to you later," I tell Ian, ending the call before he can reply. When he instantly calls back, I turn off the phone. I have to think.

Maybe the pictures were taken before we were together. I force myself to look through the photos, paying more attention to their surroundings, hoping to see some clue they're old. Preferably years.

The only thing I notice is they've all been taken outdoors. Of course, Mason is an outdoors type of guy. My tears overflow as I picture him stretched out beside the fire, his smile as he motioned for me to join him.

Ian bursts through my front door just as I spot something that steals all my hope. In the shot of him and the blond, a bank ticker shows the date and time. May 24, 3:17pm. The day after he supposedly came back to town. He must've met her when he went out for the pizza and movies while I napped. Right after he swore he wasn't seeing anyone else and called me his girlfriend. He lied. There is someone else. God, how many are there?

"Everly," Ian says softly, embracing me as I try not to cry. His concern pushes me over the edge, and I sob into his neck. I know I'm probably freaking him out. I don't think he's seen me cry since I was a kid. "Shh, whatever it is, we'll figure it out."

I let him go and shove the pictures toward him. He studies them before asking, "Where did you get these?"

"In the mail. Probably some bitch he's fucking wants him to herself."

He picks up the envelope and pulls out a white sheet of paper with one line of bold type across the top. Are you happy being one of his whores?

"Ev, you need to call the cops. This is probably the same person who smashed up your car."

"I don't care. She can have him."

"You're upset. You aren't thinking straight. I'm calling the cops. Some crazy bitch could be stalking you. She's obviously stalking him."

"And fucking him," I hiss, my anger overtaking the shock and heartache.

Ian hugs me tight. "You don't know that."

"I know he lied. He said he wasn't seeing anyone else, that all he could think about was me. And my dumb ass fell for it."

"Stop that shit." Ian holds me at arms length and his dark eyes burn into mine. "You finally put yourself out there. Maybe it won't end well this time, but I'm proud of you for trying."

My phone beeps with a message from Mason.

-Miss you already beautiful.-

Fucking son of a bitch! It's a wonder my screen doesn't crack as I type my return message.

-Take me off the list of bitches you sent that message to.-

I quickly take a picture of each of the photos and attach them to the message before sending it. A few minutes pass, and he starts ringing my phone. After the second time I send it to my voicemail, Ian snatches it and accepts the call. "She doesn't want to talk to you." Ian moves to the kitchen table, rubbing his temple as Mason talks. Part of me wants to hear his side even though it won't change anything.

"She's safe. You're the one being followed. I called the cops." After listening to his response, Ian snorts. "She'll never go for that. Yeah, I'll tell her. You need to straighten this shit out, man. You're breaking her heart."

Damn it Ian! I flop across from him, shaking my head vehemently and reaching for the phone. He easily dodges my attempts and tells Mason, "Let me know what you find out."

I glare at him as he ends the call and hands me my phone. "Making a new friend?"

"Shut up, Ev. You aren't taking this out on me. He needed to know someone was following him. He's worried you're in danger and wants to hire a security team."

"I don't need his hired goons following me. Why does he give a shit anyway? Did he even try to deny he was with those girls?"

"He said it isn't what it looks like, and to please call him when you're ready for him to explain."

"When hell's a glacier." A knock at the door interrupts our conversation, and I go to file another police report.

I've stayed at Ian's apartment for nearly a week. Mason called and texted a few times the first three days, then gave up. I'm not surprised. I'm sure he's on to the next gullible woman. To top it all off, Amy left for New York last night. Anger has propelled me through my week. Anger at Mason for being a liar, anger at myself for falling for it, anger at the world for being unfair.

Ian insists I stay one more night, and I know he's still worried over who sent the pictures. I'm sure it was just another woman who wants him, and when she sees we have no contact, she'll leave me alone.

Alone is all I want to be right now, because as the anger fades, pain seeps in. I miss him. I feel like a psycho, arguing with myself in my head. I miss him. I hate him. He can be so sweet. He's a lying, cheating asshole. Maybe I should let him explain. Maybe I should throw something at his junk.

I'm driving myself crazy and I need to be alone to sort through the swarm of feelings bombarding me. But arguing with Ian is like running uphill in flip flops. Uncomfortable, exhausting, and pointless. So I agree to one more night.

"Hey, Ev," Ian greets me, dropping his briefcase on the table. "Have a good day?"

"Pretty good." I do my best to sound upbeat. "BTC needed another volunteer to take the kids to The Children's Museum. Then we went to the go-cart track. I totally kicked ass." It was a fun day. I did my best not to be depressed in front of the kids, but Danny noticed my mood and asked about it. He backed off quick when I snapped at him to mind his own business. That was the last time he questioned me about "boyfriend trouble". "How was your day?"

Ian smiles, stripping off his tie and unbuttoning his shirt cuffs. "I got this hot chick's number at lunch."

"Of course you did. I'll head home tonight, and you can get laid. I'm fine, Ian."

"I'll call her tomorrow. Tonight we're binge watching Supernatural on Netflix and eating our weight in tacos. So get to cooking."

I smack him on the arm as he tries to dodge me. "Since you

asked so nicely."

"I'm always nice."

The rattle of pots and pans echoes through the house as I hunt for a decent skillet, and Ian heads off to shower and change. He sucks down half a dozen tacos, but I only manage one. Apparently, my appetite receded along with my anger.

"Hey, turn back to the news," I tell Ian as he channel surfs. The headline story is the capture of The Naked Bandits. Apparently, the FBI was one step ahead of them, and now they're all under arrest. Was it less than a month ago that I stood naked in that bank, humiliated while Mason protected me from the bandits and other prying eyes? He's become important to me so fast.

"At least no one got hurt," Ian remarks, and I grunt noncommittally. I'm hurt.

After a few hours of watching Sam and Dean salt and burn the bones, I'm done. I've hardly paid them the attention they deserve anyway. When I turn to tell Ian I'm going to bed, he doesn't give me the chance. His warm arms embrace me and to my horror, I instantly start crying.

He tightens his hold when I try to pull away. "It's okay, pup. Okay to miss him. Okay to be upset."

"It's not. I've known him less than a month. It's ridiculous."

"It's enough time to know you love someone and mourn the loss of it."

My arms lock around his waist and I rest my head on his shoulder. "I don't love him."

"Okay."

"I just want to forget him. It was a mistake. Now I can't go back to Striking Back."

"I talked to him today. He's leaving town tomorrow for a few days. He won't show up at Striking Back."

At least I can say goodbye to everyone. I sit up and glare at Ian. "Why are you talking to him?"

"He wanted to know if you'd gotten any more threats. He's still trying to track down who did it." Ian's voice softens. "He's waiting to hear from you. For what it's worth, he sounds miserable."

"It's worth nothing. Whose side are you on?" I demand, furious he's defending him.

"Yours, honey. Always yours. Come on, let's go to bed. You can sleep with me tonight. I'll cuddle you if you can keep your hands to yourself."

"That's got to be the first time you've said that to a girl," I snort.

Wrapped in Ian's warm arms, I feel better, a little less lonely. But as I drift off to sleep I dream of thick biceps covered in tattoo flowers.

I wake with a new determination to get on with my life. It's not the first time I've had my heart broken. Maybe someday I'll actually learn from it. Ian makes me promise to call him every day when he drops me at my apartment.

At least I have my book group as a distraction. I don't want to spend any more time thinking about Mason. After a quick shower, I head to Bellini's to meet up with everyone. The back dining room is buzzing with laughter and conversation as the half lit women discuss the latest erotica book.

"The writing was awful!" Janet exclaims. "I've never seen so many adverbs."

"Who cares?" Bridgette challenges. "The sex scenes were scorching. I don't read erotica for the grammar any more than I watch Magic Mike for the stellar acting." Everyone laughs and the discussion rattles on. Marie signals for me to join her in the back, and she doesn't look happy.

"Are you okay?" I ask.

She grabs my arm and tugs me onto the patio. All the tables are empty except for one. Macy sits slumped over in her chair, her head in her hands as her elbows rest on the table. "Show her, honey. You can trust Ev."

Pitiful bloodshot eyes meet mine and I'm filled with anger at the sight of her face. Her bottom lip is split and her top is swollen and puffy. She sighs as I sit beside her. "What happened?"

"It looks worse than it is. Marie's making too much of it."

"Who hit you?"

"He's so pissed because I won't take him back."

"Al did this?"

"He calls my job all day. I've been staying with a friend, and he bangs on her door every night, then parks across the street for hours when I won't answer."

"Have you called the police?"

"No! Who knows what he'd do!" Her eyes are wide and terrified as she stands to leave. "I shouldn't have said anything."

"Stop." I grab her hand and stare her in the eye. "We aren't going to do anything you don't want us to."

"Ev, he's stalking her. He hit her. She needs to press charges," Marie insists.

"And he'll be out of jail the next day looking for her."

"Exactly," Macy sighs, relieved I understand her position.

"Is there somewhere safe you can stay tonight? You're welcome to come home with me."

"I...you don't have to do that."

"Please, let me help." I explain all about Striking Back and the services they provide. "They can protect you. Get you the legal help to keep him away from you. I work with them, and they're wonderful people. We can go in the morning."

"Thank you." She hugs me. "I feel so stupid."

"Don't. You didn't ask for this, and you were smart to leave when he got controlling. Come home with me. I'll tell you about my month. Show you the true definition of stupid." We laugh and after Macy calls her friend to bring her a change of clothes, we head to my apartment.

We're relaxing with two huge bowls of ice cream when Mason texts me.

-Evie, please call me. It's not what it looks like.-

Noting my expression, Macy asks, "Is that him?"

"Yes. I'm not calling him." It's so hard not to talk to him, but I won't let this go any further. I've been cheated on before and I won't deal with it again.

"Men are dicks. Maybe I should just be a lesbian."

"Bitches are crazy too," I point out.

We're up early the next morning and Macy is a bundle of

nerves as we step through the back door of Striking Back. "It'll be okay," I reassure her, squeezing her hand.

I called to explain her situation, and Ms. Den is waiting for her to arrive. "You have my number," I remind her. "Call me anytime." After we share a quick hug, Ms. Den sweeps her away to get settled. I spend the next few hours with the residents, laughing and chatting, playing a board game with the kids. I want to make the most of it. After all, this may be the last time I get to spend time here.

Just as I'm about to leave, Mason texts again.

-I'm leaving town for a few days. I've tried to give you some space, but we're going to talk when I return. I miss you, Everly.-

A pain settles in my chest at the thought of never seeing him again, but it has to be this way. By the time he returns, I'll have said goodbye to everyone at S.B. and be on my way to getting over him.

There must be some big event going on downtown because traffic is a bitch. I cut through a narrow alley to get to my car that's parked a block away. I'm completely lost in thought when a sharp pain slices through the back of my head. "Stupid bitch," a voice growls, and I'm shoved to the ground, my body slamming into the concrete.

"What?" I'm dizzy and my confused brain can't comprehend what's happening. My eyes adjust, showing me a close up view of someone's discarded cigarette butt. When I turn my head to see my attacker, a black boot slams into my temple, and I dive into the welcome fog of unconsciousness

Voices reverberate through the mist, but I only catch bits and pieces of conversation.

"Cat scan."

"Where the fuck were you?" That sounds like Mason. What's he doing here?

"I'm sorry. I only lost sight of her for a minute."

Darkness floats over me again. When I can finally force my eyes open, my breath catches at the sight in front of me. Mason is slumped in a chair beside my bed, his long legs stretched across the floor. He's asleep with a frown on his face.

I need to sit up. My head feels full of angry hornets, fighting to escape. Just a small attempt to change position sends a wave of nausea through me and I groan as pain pierces my back. "Evie?" Mason's eyes pop open. "Don't move, love. You're hurt."

No shit. "What happened?"

The mattress sinks as he settles his big body beside me and takes my hand. "You were attacked. Do you remember anything?"

"I was walking from S.B. and someone hit me from behind."

"Did you see who it was?"

"No, my eyes were blurry."

Mason presses a hand against my shoulder when I try to sit up. "It's okay, baby. You need to be still."

Panicked, I reach between my legs, breathing a sigh of relief when I realize I'm still wearing my panties. "Attacked? Was I? Did he?"

Understanding dawns on his face and he embraces me, whispering in my ear. "No, love. He didn't touch you. Apparently, he hit you in the head more than once. He ran when someone came to help."

"I want to go home. Will you get my phone so I can call Ian?"

"He just left to get a coffee. He'll be right back, but you aren't going home. You have a concussion and two cracked ribs. They want to keep you overnight."

The memories of the last few days sweep over me. He cheated. More than once. "I appreciate you coming, Mason, but I'm okay. You don't need to stay."

"Shut up, Evie. I'm not going anywhere. Now, does anything hurt?"

"Everything hurts," I admit.

His warm lips brush my forehead. "I'll get a nurse."

My nurse is a plump pleasant older woman with a comforting smile. She adds a painkiller to my I.V. and shows me how to call for her before leaving the room. My eyes droop from the drugs, and Mason pulls the blanket over my chest.

"Rest, baby. I'll be right here beside you." As much as I hate to admit it, his reassurance is comforting. I want him beside me.

When I come to again, Ian is sitting next to me, his eyes bloodshot. "Hey, Pup. How do you feel?"

"Thirsty," I reply in a strained voice. He helps me sit up and hands me a cup of ice water.

"I'm so sorry. I never should've taken you home." His voice cracks.

I reach to squeeze his hand. "Don't, this isn't on you. I can't stay with you forever. It's not your fault some psycho attacked me."

He nods, wiping his eyes. "The cops want to talk to you when you're up to it."

"Because that's done me so much good in the past."

"We're going to find out who's doing this. I promise."

"Have them check the women in the pictures. My car was vandalized during my first date with Mason. The pictures and note were delivered after we went away for a few days. I was attacked outside his organization. It's someone he's fucking or someone he dumped."

The doubt on Ian's face pisses me off. "You don't believe me?"

"I'm not saying you're wrong. It could well be a disgruntled ex, but you need to talk to Mason, Ev. The pictures don't necessarily mean he was cheating."

Tears fill my eyes. It's too much, the pain in my head and body doesn't compare to the ache in my heart. Listening to Ian side with Mason again makes me feel like I've lost him too. "No, Everly." Ian crawls in bed beside me, careful not to pull my I.V. He guides my head gently to his chest. "I've got your back, always. You know that. You've been through a lot the past few weeks. Right now, you just need to rest. Don't worry about anything but getting better."

"I want to go home."

"I know, but it isn't safe."

"I can't keep staying with you."

"I want you to, but I won't be home during the day, and until we catch this asshole you can't be alone." He holds me tighter. "God, Everly, he could have killed you. I've never been so scared in my life. When Mason called me…"

"Wait. How did Mason know where I was?"

Mason enters with a duffel bag and answers my question. "My security detail was monitoring you."

"You had me followed?" I demand.

"I had you protected."

"They did a bang up job," I snap.

His face softens. "The guard lost you in the crowd. When he figured out you cut down the alley, he was too late. He got a brief glimpse of the man who attacked you. We'll catch him."

I bring my hands to my head, closing my eyes. It's all too much. My boyfriend was having me monitored without my permission while he was probably off with some new bitch. Someone is out to hurt me, even kill me. A wave of nausea sweeps over me and I take a deep breath. Throwing up would be excruciating right now.

"You have to take it easy, love, and let us keep you safe."

"You're sure it was a man?"

"Yes," Mason replies. "I promise he won't touch you again. I'll have security at my house around the clock."

My eyes pop open. "I'm not going home with you."

Ian sighs. "It's the safest place for you." His pleading eyes meet mine. "Please, Everly, just trust me. I'd never do anything to hurt you."

With a deep sigh, I give up. "Fine, whatever you want." I'm too exhausted and in too much pain to argue. "Will you ask the nurse if I can have something for nausea?"

"Of course." Ian scoots off the bed and plants a kiss on my forehead.

Mason sits on the edge of the bed. "I know I'm not your favorite person at the moment, Evie, but I'm just trying to do what's best for you. When I found out you were hurt, I couldn't get here fast enough. I don't really remember the drive here. Just a lot of honking and cursing."

"From you or the other drivers?"

A small smile tilts his lips and he adjusts my blanket. "A

little of both."

"You said you were leaving town."

"I was at the airport when I got the call. Parker went in my place."

"I'm sorry. This isn't your problem."

I close my eyes as his fingers sweep lightly across my forehead, brushing a strand of hair from my eyes. "You could never be a problem, Panda."

Chapter Eight

I'm allowed to leave the hospital the following evening under strict orders to stay in bed for a few days. Ian meets me at Mason's house with a bag of clothes and my phone.

"Good," Mason tells him. "You're just in time to help me get her stubborn ass into bed."

"I'll sleep in the guest room," I insist, starting down the hall. I make it about three steps before I'm scooped up and cradled against Mason's chest.

"My room has an attached bathroom. You're staying there." I don't have the strength to argue anymore as he carries me down the hall to his room.

Ian grins at me, and I flip him off while Mason places me on the bed and tugs off my shoes. Leaning to kiss my cheek, Ian puts my bag beside the bed. "I can see you're in good hands, Ev, so I'm going to go. I'll come by after work tomorrow."

"Okay," I reply, lying back. Just the trip from the hospital has left me exhausted.

"Call me if you need me. Love ya."

"Love ya."

Mason slips his fingers under the waistband of my sweats as soon as Ian's gone. "Don't." I resist, twisting away. The movement sends a sharp pain through my back.

He shakes his head at my gasp. "Evie, you're going to hurt yourself. I'm just trying to make you comfortable. You'll burn up in those sweats."

Giving in again, I allow him to remove my pants and sweatshirt. He pulls one of his t-shirts over my head and covers me with a fluffy comforter. The bed dips as he sits beside me. "Better, love?"

"Mmm Hmm, thanks." I snuggle into the bed, fighting to keep my eyes open.

"Get some sleep and we'll talk in the morning. Just call for me if you need anything."

"I will." I feel his soft lips against my forehead as my eyes slam shut.

When I wake, the room is dark and my pain is back with a vengeance. My head feels like an overinflated tire, and my back is full of needles. Mason hears my moan when I try to roll over. "You okay, baby?"

"Hurts."

"Your head?"

"And my back. Fuck, everything. I need to lie on my side, but it hurts too bad to turn over. Why am I getting worse?"

"They doped you up pretty good before we left the hospital, but that was nearly twelve hours ago. The pain meds have worn off. Lie still a minute." He dashes to the kitchen for a bottle of water, then grabs a container of pills from the bedside table. Gently, he helps me sit up and scoots to sit behind me so I can lean back against his chest while I swallow two pills.

Strong arms wrap around me and I'm surrounded by his warm scent. "Just relax and give the medicine a few minutes to work."

I can barely make out his tattoos in the dim room. "Why flowers?" I murmur.

"You don't like them?"

"They're beautiful. I just thought there may be a story behind them."

His chin rests on my shoulder as he responds. "More than one story, love. Each flower stands for something."

I trace a purple flower on his bicep. "What's this one stand for?"

"Purple hyacinths are given as an apology." Oh, what's he sorry for?

"This is a magnolia."

"Yeah, it represents perseverance and stamina."

"Well, you have no shortage of that."

His deep chuckle makes me grin. "You sure know how to test it. Are you feeling better?"

"Mmm Hmm, high as a giraffe's tit," I slur, and Mason laughs aloud. He stretches out beside me, and I lie down on my side, resting my cheek in the crook of his arm. Whew! That pill is kicking my ass. My mind is full of fog and I realize I'm falling asleep again. "I really fucked up."

"No, baby, you didn't do anything wrong."

"I fell in love with a cheater again."

Mason's side of the bed is empty when I wake. Shit. No wonder, it's nearly noon. Those pills wiped me out. I feel a little better, my head is bearable, but my whole body still aches. Slowly, I manage to make my way to the bathroom to pee. My image in the mirror is disgusting. Nearly three days without a shower has left my hair limp and oily.

A large purple bruise covers my temple, stretching from my cheekbone to my hairline. I'm grateful to find my toothbrush on the counter and waste no time brushing my teeth. After pulling my hair into a ponytail, I hear Mason call my name from the bedroom. "Coming," I reply.

"You should've waited. I'd have helped you."

"I'm okay. What's all this?" A large tray laden with food waits on the bedside table.

"You need to eat. Are you hurting?"

"Not as bad as last night." When he picks up the pill bottle, I shake my head. "I don't want knocked out again."

"Lightweight," he teases. "Put some food in your stomach

and then just take one. It won't fuck you up so bad. Then you can soak in a hot bath to help your sore muscles."

God, he's being so sweet. "Okay, look, Mason..."

"Eat, baby, then we'll talk."

"Okay."

"If only you were always this agreeable."

"Give me a day or two to recover, then you won't be able to boss me around." I laugh. Once I start eating, I realize how hungry I am and scarf down the oatmeal, toast, and banana in record time. I can hear Mason running a bath and a lump forms in my throat. He's been right beside me the whole time, just like he promised. How can he be so caring and sweet, then run to other women?

I don't argue when he pulls off my t-shirt and pushes my panties to my feet so I can step out of them. "Oh, Evie." His voice is low and tortured as he takes in the bruise stretching from my back around to the right side of my chest. Another covers my left hip.

"I'm okay." He holds my hand as I step into the hot water. The tub is massive and the water reaches my chin when I lie back. "You don't have to babysit me. I'll be fine."

"And miss out on this view? Even covered in bruises, you're stunning, Evie."

"Mason, please. You've been great, but I can't..."

"Shh. Let me show you something and explain before you finish that sentence." He produces his phone and holds it up where I can see the photo of him with his arm around a blond woman. He flips through the remaining pictures that were mailed to me, then zooms in on the blonde's face. "Look at her. Does she look happy?"

On closer inspection, I see her eyes are red and puffy. "She looks like she's been crying."

"How about here?" It's the one of Mason's hand on the shoulder of a tall brunette. "Look romantic? Like lovers in the sunshine?"

I close my eyes, soaking in the hot water as it soothes my muscles. "She looks miserable. What's your point? Are you trying to tell me your stalker caught you breaking up with your harem for me?" Does he really think that's much better?

He snorts. "No. I was never with them. You know how most of the women feel when they come to Striking Back. They're heartbroken and terrified. I meet with each woman in a public place the first time for an intake interview, somewhere they feel safe. That's what the pictures show. I'm reassuring them I can protect them."

I study the photos again. "None of these women are living at your shelter," I point out, sitting up carefully so I don't slosh water onto the floor.

Mason grabs the shampoo as I reach for it and turns on the shower attachment to wet my hair. "The blonde woman is named Tracy Long and she's at S.B. She moved in the day you were attacked. The tall woman decided she felt safer out of state so we sent her to a sister shelter in Florida."

"And the last woman?"

"Backed out and went home to her husband." His hands feel so good lathering my hair while I remain silent, thinking it through.

"You haven't been with anyone else?"

"No, baby." He gently washes my back before handing me the cloth so I can finish. "Ready to get out?"

I nod, and he takes my hand, helping me out of the tub. Before I can protest, he dries me off from head to toe with a fluffy towel and helps me dress. I wrap him in a hug. "I'm sorry I accused you."

His chin rests on my head. "I understand how it looked."

"But I don't think I can keep doing this. I just can't handle a relationship right now. I'll screw it up, and you'll end up hating me."

His large palms cup my jaws and bright blue eyes burrow into mine. "I could never hate you. This isn't easy for me either. We have the same abandonment issues. We just cope differently. You try to leave before you get left, and I hold onto to what's precious to me with all my might. I'm overprotective, and I know it can be smothering, but I don't cheat. You can trust me."

His lips part mine with the softest of kisses, and his next words tear down any remaining doubt that I'm in too deep to see out. "I love you, Everly. Please stop running from me."

My tears overflow and I can't stop them. "I'm sorry. You've been so good to me. I should've let you explain."

"It's okay, love. You've had a terrible week. Just let me take care of you. Everything will be okay. I'm right here beside you." His strong arms wrap around my waist and he leads me to the couch in the living room, already made up with pillows and a blanket. "We'll just hang out and watch movies while you rest. Ian will be coming by in a few hours."

"Mason." I grab his arm, pulling him down beside me before he can walk away. "I love you, too." His eyes light up and a wide smile blooms across his face. He pulls me into his lap, kissing me in that long slow way I love, and I feel something inside me loosen and relax. I'm in love with him. He loves me. We'll be okay. We spend the next few days together while I recover.

Mason settles in beside me on the couch, a worried expression on his face. "Everly, I need to talk to you about something. I was going to wait until you were well, but I think you need to know."

Turning to press my back against the arm of the couch, I pull my knees to my chest. This doesn't sound like good news.

Mason scoots closer, refusing to allow me to put any space between us. "Since the night your car was vandalized, I've had my...people investigating."

"Why didn't you tell me?"

"Not everything they do is strictly legal. I didn't want to involve you. I have friends who've worked in Military Intelligence and for Homeland Security."

"Hackers?"

"Professionals. Anyway, they discovered something. It's about your father."

"What about him?"

"Sweetheart...he's not dead."

I laugh at the absurdity of it. "What the hell are you talking about? I've seen his death certificate, been to his grave."

"The U.S. Marshals helped him fake his death. He's in the Witness Protection Program." He slips his hand into mine and stares into my eyes. "He's alive, Evie."

My head is spinning. There has to be some mistake. "Why, though? Who's after him?"

Mason lowers his head. "From the information I have, it could be a number of people." His reluctance to tell me is stamped on his face, but with a sigh, he says, "Your father was a Mob boss. The car accident was an attempt on his life."

"No, he would've taken me into Witness Protection with him. There must be some mistake."

"Maybe he thought you'd be safer with a new family. Where you wouldn't be connected with him if he were found."

"So, he left me? The money!" I cry, realizing what all this means. "He sent me the money. It wasn't an inheritance. God, Mason, I'm living on dirty Mob money!"

"You don't know that, baby. I'm sure he wanted to know you'd always be taken care of." Mason embraces me, but I can't stop shaking. My father can't be alive. And the Mob? Christ, it's like something out of a bad movie.

I don't know what to do with this information. I don't even remember him, really. Just a vague picture of a dark headed man with my eyes. "What am I supposed to do?"

"You don't have to do anything. I just wanted you to know. I don't want you to fight me on security. You being targeted probably has nothing to do with your father, but we need to be sure. You can't be alone until we figure out who's behind this. And I will, Everly. I'll take care of it."

"I just…I don't want to think about this right now."

"Okay. Just rest. We'll talk about it when you're ready."

After three days, I feel much better. The dizziness and headache are gone. My ribs will take longer to heal, but the pain is manageable. "Go to work, Mason. I swear I won't leave the house." It's the third time I've tried to convince him. I feel bad he's missing work because of me.

"Tell you what, I'm supposed to teach a children's class at four, followed by a private sparring lesson at five-thirty. Come with me and watch."

"You don't want to be seen with me like this, with big ugly bruises. I'll embarrass you." My black eye has turned an unattractive greenish yellow.

His fingers pinch my chin and he stares me in the eye. "You're begging for me to spank that sweet little ass of yours, Evie. I'd never be embarrassed by you. You're coming with me."

My hands seem to have a mind of their own, sliding to squeeze his firm ass. "Hmm, I think there's a deal to be made here."

Lust darkens his eyes as he grinds his hips into mine. Finally! He's been totally hands off since I got out of the hospital. "A deal, huh?"

"Don't worry, it's a win-win. I hang out at your gym today." A low groan rumbles his chest as I rub my fingers over his crotch. "And you give me a workout tonight."

He dips his head, his breath warming my ear and murmurs, "You aching for it, Evie? Aching for my cock inside you?"

"Since the second you pulled it out of me."

He closes his eyes. "Fuck. You can't say things like that when I can't fuck your brains out."

"You started it," I tease, trying to slow my breathing.

"Get ready to go, baby. I promise to make you scream tonight."

Reed's gym is much bigger and nicer than I expected. I pictured a stinky sweaty room with a boxing ring and a few punching bags. "This place is great," I exclaim, squeezing Mason's hand as he leads me inside. It's a large open floor half covered by mats. A floor to ceiling mirror runs the length of one wall, making the room appear even larger. A few rows of chairs are tucked into one corner, waiting for the parents of his students.

I'm led past the mats where two men in sparring gear are fighting. "Point! Try me again, brother. You're still leaving yourself open with that back leg roundhouse." I laugh as I recognize the two guys when they remove their helmets, jogging toward us.

"Hey, how are you feeling, honey?" Alex asks me, studying my bruised face.

"It looks worse than it feels. I'm good."

"He's going to be in his own hell when we find him," Parker assures me. Their concern touches me. They barely know me. "We can cover your schedule, bro. You don't have to be here."

"Evie wanted to watch me whip some ass today," Mason says, showing me to a leather couch in the corner. He turns to his brothers. "Keep an eye on her while I'm teaching."

"Yeah," I scoff. "I may wander off and stick a penny in an electrical socket."

"You do like to put things in your mouth," Mason teases with a smirk, and I smack him. "Just stay close to one of them, okay? So I don't have to worry."

"I'll be good and stay in the yard, I promise." I drop a quick kiss on his lips as his students start trickling through the door. "Go do your thing."

Parker and Alex sit on either side of me while Mason greets his students and chats with the parents. "Fuck me, who's the new MILF?" Parker asks, staring at a tall slender redheaded woman.

"Don't even think about it, Park. Mason will beat the shit out of you," Alex warns.

"Why would Mason care who he hits on?"

"Because he's a tramp and when he screws the mother, then moves on, we lose a student."

Parker holds up his hands. "I make it clear from the jump I'm just looking for some fun."

"Yeah, well, they don't get the joke." Alex shakes his head, reminding me of Mason. They all share that response when they're frustrated or amused. "We lost three students last year, not to mention that psycho woman smashing our window."

"Shut the fuck up. You'll give Everly the wrong idea about

me. She'll never hook me up with her friends." Parker scoots closer to me, flashing a sideways grin I'm sure usually gets him his way. "Are your best friends hot, Ev? Want to introduce me?"

Alex grins at me as I laugh. "My best friend is definitely hot. Dark brown eyes and thick gorgeous hair. Ass you could take a bite out of."

"Holy shit. Single? You want to hook me up?"

"I'll ask, but I don't think Ian's into guys. You might get lucky, though." Alex laughs aloud, throwing an arm around my shoulder.

Parker smirks. "Great. A smartass. You'll fit right in around here. Stay with her, Alex. I'm going to meet Ms. Perky Tits." He bounds from the couch and saunters over to sit beside the woman, flashing a charming smile.

When she blushes and smiles back, Alex groans, "There goes another one."

"Has he always been that way?"

"A woman screwed him over when he was young. It's no excuse, but since then, it's been a revolving door of pissed off ladies." I wonder if Mason whored around before we got together, but I know his brother would never tell me.

My gaze wanders to Mason, standing in front of the mirrors, demonstrating kicks and punches to a room of eight year olds. They gaze at him, held rapt by his authoritative nature. He's in his element, joy shining in his eyes as he does what he loves.

Alex laughs. "You've got it bad, honey."

"What?"

"Uh huh. You can't take your eyes off him," he teases, making my face heat. "He's the same with you. It's a delight to see."

"He can be a bossy bastard, but I think I'll keep him."

"Something tells me you can handle him," Alex says with a laugh.

"Tell me about your boyfriend. Is he cute?"

Alex's eyes light up. "Cooper is great. We've only been dating a few weeks, but I really like him. He's funny and sexy. A bit on the bossy side too."

"I'd love to meet him."

"We'll have to plan a night. I've met his family, so he's pushing to meet mine."

"Mason told me about your mom. I'm sorry. I know what it's like to lose a parent so young."

"Thank you. Mason had as big a hand in raising Parker and me as our aunt and uncle did. I don't know what we'd have done without him."

"Can I ask what happened to your dad?"

Alex gazes at me with regret, the corners of his mouth tucked in. "There's a long story there with a bad ending. Mason should be the one to tell it. Give him time, though. He hates to talk about it."

"Sure."

Mason dismisses his class and joins us on the sofa. "What are you talking about?"

"Just telling her all your secrets."

"So, does he still wet the bed?" I ask, turning to Alex.

"I think he outgrew it."

Mason slaps him in the back of the head and he jogs away, laughing.

I cuddle into his side. "Your brother is really nice."

"I take it you mean, Alex."

"Parker's nice too, but he's kind of a pig."

"No 'kind of' about it, love. I've got a half hour sparring match. Will you be okay? Is your back hurting?" He runs a hand down my spine.

"I'm fine. Go kick some ass."

Mason strips off his t-shirt and winks at me while he tightens up his gloves. I'm glad to see him put on headgear, though it won't protect his handsome face.

The guy Mason is sparring with is a little shorter and kind of skinny. I learn quickly that thin and wiry also means fast. His punches and kicks are a blur. Mason taps gloves with him, congratulating him for getting a punch through. He seriously laughed and praised the man for punching him in the face. These guys are crazy.

I focus on Mason's body to distract from the ache that tightens my stomach when I see him get hit. The way he moves, so graceful yet aggressive, is mesmerizing. Broad shoulders give way to a perfectly sculpted chest, lightly dusted with hair. I remember how soft it felt against my cheek when I rested on him.

Sweat trickles down to his toned abs, running between the defined muscles and soaking into the waistband of his shorts. His back flexes as he lands another punch, knocking the other guy on his ass.

When he bends to offer his hand to help him up, my eyes are drawn to the dimples in his lower back. I'm so going to lick them next time he's naked. The match ends with Mason showing the man some counterstrikes and suggesting moves he should work on before his next match.

I just want to get him home so he can use those graceful moves on me.

Mason laughs and pulls me into bed with him when I admit I don't like watching him fight. "I cringed every time the guy landed a punch."

"He didn't hurt me, baby, but I love that you worry about me."

"Could you watch someone punch me in the face?"

"I'd kill them." He brushes a strand of hair from my forehead. "Seeing you hurt like this tears me apart."

"I'm okay. I believe we had a deal, Mr. Reed." I strip off my clothes and reach to pull off his shorts.

"Oh no you don't. We're doing this my way tonight."

"And what's your way?"

"You're going to lay back and do what I tell you. And I'm going to make you come until you lose your voice."

I've already lost my words. Anything I say will just come out as nonsensical babbling. Mason's devious grin shows he recognizes the effect he's having on me. I scoot up the bed and lie back, tucking my hands behind my head.

Mason crawls up my body and murmurs in my ear. "Good girl. I don't want to hurt your ribs, so relax and let me love you."

Warmth washes over me when he runs his tongue down my belly, dipping it into my navel. "I'm going to take my time with you, Evie. You're going to beg me to fuck you." His words enflame me almost as much as the sensation of his fingers sinking into me. Curling them, he massages the spot that simultaneously shuts off my brain and drives me insane, grinning when I groan. "Tell me when you're close, baby."

The next few minutes are filled with constant pleasure and unbearable torment. I get right to the edge so many times just to have the feeling abate as he lightens his strokes. "Mason…please." I twist away from him. "Just fuck me."

Gently, he scoops me up to straddle his lap. His eyes sparkle with mischief as they stare into mine. "Just can't hold still, can you?" His fingers resume stroking me inside and out, faster and faster. I'm overcome with heat and I can feel the first pulses of my release begin. I also really have to pee. Like bad.

"Mason, stop. I need the bathroom."

"No, you don't love. Trust me. Relax your muscles. Let it go."

Suddenly, I'm gripped by the most powerful orgasm of my life. It tears through me, spreading out from my sex, racing to every inch of my body. I hear myself scream as another wave crashes through me, and I tear my eyes open in time to see a blast of liquid soak Mason's hand.

He doesn't stop and the spasms go on and on. When they fade, I fall forward on his chest, swallowing hard and fighting to catch my breath. "Don't let go of me." His arms tighten around my back while I bury my face in his neck. "Fuck. I didn't think I could do that."

His chuckle makes me sit back, and I feel his hard cock beneath me. He grabs my hips when I rise to take him in. "No, baby, you'll hurt yourself riding me. Lay on your belly."

Trying to ignore the huge wet spot on the bed, I scoot over

and stretch out on my stomach. Mason's firm hand runs down my back, then lifts my hips to slide a pillow beneath them, raising my ass a few inches. "So fucking sexy," he murmurs, and I gasp as he smacks the curve of my ass. "You like that?" He spanks the other cheek, and I'm mortified at the groan that escapes my throat.

"Oh, Evie, so naughty. I can't wait to put you over my knee when you're healed. Right now, I'm going to take you." He buries himself completely, making me cry out as I stretch to accommodate his size. My neck and back are covered with passionate open mouthed kisses as he fucks me in long slow strokes. Within minutes, I'm coming again, and this time he joins me, groaning into my neck.

Collapsing beside me, he cuddles me close, entwining our limbs. God, sex with this man just gets better and better. After a few minutes, he kisses my neck and heads to the bathroom, returning with a warm washcloth.

I have to look away when he spreads me open, running the wet cloth between my legs. "Evie," he teases, "You let me spank you, and spray all over my hand, but this is too intimate?"

"Shut up. I didn't let you. You just did it."

"I'll do it again, too." I curl into his side, planting my face in the crook of his arm so he can't see the heat in my face. "Don't hide from me, love. There's no reason to be embarrassed, or hide what feels good. You can be anyone you want with me; my naughty girl, my princess, my brave fighter. I want to know you. All of you. Every angle and nuance of that beautiful brain and firm little body. I want all of you, Evie."

"Do I get all of you in return?"

"What you see is all of me. I'm not that complicated."

"Will you tell me what happened to your dad?"

Mason sighs. "He's in prison. I really don't like to talk about it."

Holy shit. I didn't see that coming. He looks so unhappy I can't question him further though I'm dying to know what crime his father committed. "Okay, just one more question, then."

The corners of his mouth tuck in, showing his reluctance. "Go ahead."

"Where did you learn to fuck like that?"

A relieved laugh fills the room. "I grew up with my aunt and uncle who were…well, hippies. They taught a weekly tantric sex class, and my brothers and I may have eavesdropped a few times on the lesson plan."

Chapter Nine

The police have turned up nothing in my attack, and Mason's investigators have drawn a blank as well. Mason stays stitched to my hip for the next week. He and Ian insist I stay with him until the guy is caught. Amy agrees. "Jesus, girl, I can't leave you for a fucking second, you're trying to get yourself killed," she says, nearly yelling into her phone.

"I'm fine, Amy. How are things going? Do you like New York? How is Wendy?"

"New York's amazing, things are great, and Wendy and I are fine. Are you staying close to the tattoo god?"

"His name is Mason. And yes, I'm staying with him. The Striking Back waterpark and carnival is tomorrow, so don't worry if you can't get a hold of me."

"All right, chick. I have to get to work. Call me if you need me."

"I will." I end the call and flop back on the couch. It's been wonderful spending all this time with Mason. We've been out to dinner and the movies, spent hours curled up on the couch talking.

I love being with him, but I don't want him spending time with me because he's forced to, just because I'm in danger. After tomorrow, I'll hire my own security and go back home. I can't hide forever.

The day of the carnival and waterpark trip dawns bright

and sunny. The temperature is supposed to top out at eighty-five degrees, a perfect day for swimming. As soon as I step out of Mason's car, I'm seized by the waist and pulled against his hard body.

"What are you doing?"

He steps back into an alcove, taking me with him. "Getting a taste of you before we're surrounded by impressionable kids." His lips take mine in a powerful, skin tingling kiss while he squeezes my ass with both hands.

"You'll just have to behave yourself."

"I'll do my best. Come on, you've been spotted," he says with a laugh.

Jamie flies across the pavement, pigtails bouncing. "Ev-ly! I got a new swimsuit," she cries, spinning in place in her pink striped one piece. "You like it?"

"It's almost as pretty as you. Are you ready to play in the water?"

"Yep. Are you going to play with us?" Her little friend Samantha runs up and grabs her hand.

"Hurry up, Jamie. It's our turn!"

"Go have fun, girls. I'll see you in a little bit." Sarah glances from me to Mason and smiles before leading the girls inside.

Once inside the park, we see the group from BTC splashing in the kid's area. Matty spots Mason and waves excitedly. "Mr. Reed!" he calls, running to us. "I brought a ball. Want to play?"

I grin at Mason. "Let's spend a little time with the kids first. Then we'll make our escape." Mason plays ball with the boys while I join Sarah, Jamie, and Samantha on the kiddie slides. After an hour or so, I hear an announcement calling everyone to the picnic area for lunch. Mason has arranged to have pizza delivered for everyone, and the kids can't get there fast enough.

As I'm wrapping a towel around me, firm hands land on my hips. "Come float in the lazy river with me. We'll have it all to ourselves." Goosebumps race across my neck as Mason kisses just below my ear.

"Are you going to take advantage of me?"

"I'll do my best."

He grabs an oversized innertube and settles into it before pulling me down to recline on his lap. The tube dips and sways, making me squeal as it nearly tips over before stabilizing under our weight. I laugh, lying back on his chest as we're carried along the current. When I look up at him, he takes my mouth in a soft but demanding kiss. Carefully, I twist to bury my fingers in his damp hair.

He tastes amazing and I can't resist dragging my tongue down his neck and across his chest. "You smell so good, Evie," he moans, running his nose up my cheek.

"It's the sunblock. They should make a perfume with that scent."

"No, baby, it's just you."

I burrow my face into his neck, wallowing in his affection, breathing in the scent of his skin. A combination of chlorine, sunshine, and sweat that makes me want to say to hell with the waterpark, and drag him home to bed.

As soon as we float into a long blue tunnel, he grabs my lips with his and kisses me until we run out of air. His hands roam my bikini clad body, one running across my breasts, the other slipping between my legs. "Mason..."

"No one can see us in here." Any further objections are forgotten when he pushes aside the crotch of my bottoms and strokes in just the right spot. It takes less than a minute to reach the end of the tunnel, and he quickly wraps his arms back around my waist.

"Tease."

"I couldn't look at you in that bikini any longer without touching you."

"Now I'm all worked up."

"Tonight, I'll make it all worth it." We both laugh when my stomach gives a loud growl. "I'll go grab us some lunch and we can eat by the wave pool," he offers.

"Sounds good. I'll return the innertube and meet you there." I hop out, and he follows me out of the lazy river, delivering a quick smack on my ass before heading off.

I take my time walking to the wave pool. It feels so strange to be surrounded by empty slides and lounge chairs. This place usually has thousands of people waiting in line for the attractions. There are less than one hundred here today and they're all in the picnic area, even the lifeguards. The shimmering pool with its gentle waves calls to me. Really, when will I ever have another chance to swim in it alone? Warm water laps at my legs as I wade in until it's deep enough to swim. When I reach the far edge, I roll to float on my back.

Sunshine pours over my skin, warming me from head to toe, and I relax, allowing the waves to slowly take me back toward the shore. My eyes are closed, my mind filled with thoughts of Mason and how much fun we have together.

His bossy tendencies can get a little frustrating, but his loving, affectionate ways more than compensate. He loves me. I've never been happier.

A shadow falls across my face and before I can open my eyes, a hand shoves me underwater. It only takes a second to register what's happening and for panic to set in. The water is only five feet deep and I struggle to get my feet under me. When I feel the concrete on my soles, I push as hard as I can and my head breaks the surface.

I have just enough time to take a small breath before a hand tightens in my hair, nearly tearing it out. "I gave you every chance. You bitches. Always want the rich assholes," a voice growls, and I'm shoved under again.

I try so hard not to panic, not to scream, but this is my worst nightmare come true. I'm back in the car. Water pours through the windows and I can't get my seatbelt off. I scream at Mommy and Daddy, but they won't wake up. Blood coats Mommy's hair, and I remember how it swirls pink in the water. I scream until I can't breathe. I can't breathe. I CAN'T BREATHE.

The world grows hazy and dim until my lungs no longer feel like they're full of lava. Someone is calling my name, and I hear choking and retching. It takes a second to realize it's me, and I finally draw enough air to scream.

Cool, wet skin presses against mine. "No, Evie. You're okay. I've got you. Open your eyes." The sight of Mason's ocean blue gaze instantly makes me cry. He cradles me against his chest for a moment. "You're okay. I'm right here beside you. You're going to be fine, but I need you to go with Alex a minute."

"No." I feel safe in his arms, but he hands me over to Alex, who holds me close and carries me out of the pool. I see why when I look back. Mason is beating the shit out of whoever tried to drown me. Blood mixes with the water and I close my eyes against the childhood flashbacks.

Alex places me on his lap and wraps a towel around my shoulders, consoling me while I cry. "It's over, Everly. Everything will be okay." Mason drags the bloody, unconscious man to the shore and signals to Alex. "Come on, honey. You need to see if you recognize who attacked you."

My legs are weak and shaky as I'm lead closer to the man who's been stalking me. "Is he dead?" Please say Mason didn't kill him. He'll go to prison.

"No, but he'll wish he was," Mason says, taking my hand and leading me closer.

My chest rises on a gasp, sending a sharp pain through my lungs. "Danny."

"Who is he, Evie?" Mason asks.

"Danny Fennel, a counselor at Building Tomorrow's Child. You met him for a second at Matty's birthday party. He asked me out a few times." I stare at his lifeless form in disbelief. "Why?"

"Cops are on their way," Parker says, jogging up to join us. "You okay, Everly?"

No, I'm not okay. Right now I'm really, really pissed. This asshole has attacked me twice, just because I wouldn't date him?

"Whoa!" Parker yells when I kick Danny in the ribs as hard as I can. Not the smartest move when you're wearing water shoes. Parker laughs, and Mason scoops me up before I can kick again.

"That's enough. You'll hurt yourself. The cops are coming," Mason warns.

Less than an hour later, Danny has been arrested and I'm sitting on a lounge chair, surrounded by the Reed brothers. Mason kisses my forehead and murmurs, "Let's get you home."

"No, I'm good. I don't want to let him ruin another day. I

want to go to the carnival with you tonight. He's not making me miss out on a funnel cake."

Alex chuckles and kisses my cheek before getting to his feet. "This one's a keeper, Mason." He turns to Parker. "Let's leave them alone."

My gaze alternates between them. "Thank you so much. Both of you."

"Anytime, Everly," Parker replies with a grin. "You're Mason's girl. You're one of us. Better get used to it."

They walk off, leaving us alone. "You saved me," I murmur, laying a palm against Mason's cheek.

"I never should've left you alone."

"You can't be with me every minute."

"We'll see about that." He plants a soft kiss on my lips. "You're shaking. Are you cold?"

"No, just need to sit down a minute." The scrape of plastic on concrete makes me wince as he pulls a two person lounger into the shade.

"Come here."

I take his hand and stretch out beside him, resting my head on his shoulder. I must be exhausted because it's late afternoon when I wake. Mason's covered me with a beach towel, and he sits a few feet away, talking on his phone.

He's breathtaking with the sun pouring over his shoulders, highlighting every line and muscle of that incredibly toned body. How the hell did I get lucky enough to win the affection of such a man? A wide smile appears when he sees me staring at him, and he ends his call. "Hey, sleepyhead. Feeling better?"

"Much. What did I miss?"

I hear Calliope music in the air as he answers, "Not a thing. The carnival is just starting. Do you feel up to it?"

"Absolutely. I need to grab a shower and dress. My stuff is in a locker." I hop up and stretch my sore muscles. "Meet you back here?"

I'm presented with a look that says I'm one twist short of a slinky. "You aren't going anywhere without me."

"Danny's in jail. It's over."

"You've taken years off my life the past few weeks, Evie. I'm not letting you out of my sight." He wraps an arm around my waist and we start toward the lockers.

"You just want to watch me shower," I tease.

"Guilty."

The sun is just dipping below the horizon when we enter the carnival, hand in hand. "Where to first?" Mason asks.

"Food. I'm starving."

Mason chuckles. "Lead the way, baby."

After pigging out on corndogs and funnel cake, which Mason insists on paying for, we stroll down the midway. "Race you," I dare, gesturing to the Fire Fight game. I loved this game when I was a kid. The object is to aim a stream of water through a target, which moves your wooden fire truck to the finish line.

Mason grins and grabs the water hose. "If I win, you have to go through the haunted house with me."

"Damn, I really wanted to see the haunted house, but there's no way I can lose."

The bell rings and everyone focuses on their targets. Leave it to me to choose the hose with a wussy little stream. Mason pulls ahead of me instantly, but we both laugh when the two little girls beside us leave our fire trucks in the dust.

The younger girl cheers when she wins, and the young man tending the game hands her a stuffed animal. He smiles and gives the other girl a large lollipop, and they both run away laughing and happy.

"Looks like you get to see the haunted house after all."

"You didn't win!" I smack his arm, and he grabs me by the waist.

"I beat you. You chickening out?"

"Never. I can't wait to get you alone in the dark."

Mason grins, his face lit by the colored lights. Grabbing my hand, he leads me to the haunted house ride. A young man checks our wristbands and ushers us into a car, pulling the safety bar across our laps. After warning us to keep our arms inside the car, he sends us down the track.

We make a sharp right turn through a wall of rubber strips

into pitch darkness. The car makes a few abrupt turns until I'm a little disoriented, unable to tell what direction we're going. I jump when a loud siren blares and a strobe light flashes on a man hanging from a noose, his feet kicking the side of the car. Mason laughs and slides his arm around my shoulders.

We laugh and tease each other as we travel through a room of zombies, and another set up to look like a butcher shop, littered with dismembered limbs. The car makes another turn and we're face to face with an evil looking clown. Mason stiffens up and curses under his breath as the bloody clown with a too wide grin reaches toward us.

It's my turn to laugh at his reaction. "You're scared of clowns. Don't worry," I tease, cuddling into him. "I won't let big bad Bozo get you."

Mason pinches my nipple, making me squeal, and says, "Look up, love."

A giant spider creeps across the ceiling to a web full of tiny spiders. I know they're fake, but every inch of my skin crawls at the sight of them. Suddenly, a few of the spiders rain down on us just as we travel through an archway laced with spiderwebs. The spiders falling on me and the feel of the silky strings clinging to my face and hair have me beating at myself like a mad woman.

Mason's laughter echoes through the ride, and I smack him on the chest as the car bursts into the night air. "Souvenir?" he asks, still chuckling while he holds up one of the plastic spiders.

It's a damn ring, and in the light, it couldn't look more fake. "Asshole," I grumble as he slides the ring on my finger and we exit the ride.

"Where to next?" he asks, sliding his hand in the back pocket of my jeans.

I give him a wide smile when I spot the fun photo exhibit. Multiple wooden characters are scattered about, the faces cut out so we can poke ours through and become a cowboy, or a princess, or a zombie. "Let's pick one!" I drag him through the display until I see one that was seemingly made for us. Two giant panda bears hug, a trail of hearts bubbling up between them. "What are you doing?" I ask when I notice Mason glancing around.

"Making sure my brothers aren't around. I'd never hear the end of this." He pulls me behind the wooden cutout. "Come on, Panda." We poke our faces through the holes and a man takes our picture.

"You can pick it up at the counter," he advises us, pointing us in the right direction. While we wait for our picture, Mason spots a photo booth.

"You got your picture. Now I want mine," he says, leading me into the booth and pulling the curtain. "Ready?" he asks, feeding a few dollars into the machine. It takes four photos, ten seconds apart.

I press my cheek to Mason's for the first one, and he wraps me in a hug for the second. His lips land on mine a second before the third flash. Before I realize what he's doing, he pulls up my sweatshirt, showing my bare tits to the camera just as the last click sounds. "Mason!"

"That one's for my wallet," he says with a roguish grin. We step out of the booth and almost collide with Alex. A cute athletic man stands beside him, holding his hand.

"Everly." Alex greets me with a smile. "You having a good time?"

"It's been fun. We're just waiting for our photos to process." I glance toward the slot where the pictures will be delivered.

Alex looks a bit reluctant as he introduces his boyfriend. "Cooper, this is my brother, Mason, and his girlfriend, Everly."

"Such a pretty name," Cooper says, shaking my hand.

"Thank you. It's nice to meet you." A small dimple dents his cheek as he grins at me. Oh, yeah, I can see why Alex likes him. He's a cutie.

"Nice to meet you," Mason agrees, shaking his hand.

Abruptly, the machine clicks and our photos drop into the slot. Alex picks them up, a mischievous grin breaking across his face as he peeks at them before handing them to me. "Glad to see we aren't the only ones having fun with the photo booth."

"See what you did!" I smack Mason on the arm, and he shrugs. The photo center worker chooses that moment to bring us our panda photo, and I waste no time holding it up for Alex and Cooper to see. Payback is a bitch.

Alex snorts, laughing until his eyes are full of tears. "That's fantastic, Ev. I need a copy, please."

"You got it."

Mason shakes his head, and we say goodbye to Alex and Cooper. I glance back as they climb into the photo booth. I can only imagine the amount of inappropriate pictures that booth will take tonight. Mason slides his arm around me, tucking me against his side, and I yawn. "You ready to go, love?"

"Yeah, I've had a great time, but I'm done in." Mason leads me to his car and we head back to his house. It's been such a great day, I don't want to dampen his mood by announcing I'm going home tomorrow. I'll tell him in the morning.

As Mason shuts his front door behind us, I wrap my arms around his waist, stepping into his warm body, and he holds me tight. "Attempted drowning aside, it was a wonderful day."

His chest vibrates with a deep chuckle. "You make my days wonderful, Evie."

"I love you."

"I love you, baby." His bright eyes meet mine as he releases me. "I need to make a few calls, then we'll go to bed, okay?"

"Sure. Can I borrow your laptop to check my email? My phone's dead."

"Of course. It's in my office."

I've never been in his home office before. A large cherry wood desk sits near the far wall. The room is warm and inviting. A crimson colored sofa and armchair provide a splash of color among the dark wooden furniture and flooring.

His laptop rests on his desk, and I turn it on. Curiosity gets the best of me while I wait for it to boot up. He thinks my father's alive. There must be paperwork, reports or something that shows why. I've barely had time to consider that with all that's happened.

With a quick glance at the door, I open the left hand desk drawer. It's filled with pens, pencils, and general office supplies. I can hear Mason on the phone in the living room, so I still have time. The right drawer contains a few file folders, marked with six digit numbers. On top of them is a plain white envelope.

When I pick it up, the flap opens and the contents spill onto my lap and slide to the floor. I've heard the expression 'my blood ran cold' but never understood it until now. I feel as if I've been dipped in liquid nitrogen and the smallest move will shatter me into a thousand sharp pieces.

Passports, at least a dozen, all with women's pictures. Social Security cards, driver's licenses, birth certificates. What the fuck is this? What kind of business is he running?

He's still on the phone, and I creep to the door to eavesdrop. "Got three girls, clothes on their backs. Going to need a runner. No...no, it has to be tonight. I text you the address. Yeah, same deal, twenty-five grand each. Call me when it's done."

Oh God. Oh Fuck. Money for women, fake documents. He's not saving women, he's selling them. Human trafficking. That's how he makes his money. What kind of monster have I been seeing? I have to get out of here. Who knows what he'll do to me if he knows I found out.

He ends his call, and I know there's no time to clean up the evidence. Panicking, I kick it all under the desk and dart from the office, closing the door behind me. "Hey, you ready for bed?" Mason approaches me, and I do my best not to stiffen up when he embraces me. I can't let on anything is wrong.

"Sure, just let me grab a glass of water."

His whole face is a question mark when he steps back and regards me. "Everything okay?"

"Of course, it's just been a long day. Go get naked. I'll join you in a minute."

"Hurry," he whispers, squeezing my ass.

I have to swallow the urge to vomit. How many women has he stolen? How many sent to be raped on the other side of the world? No wonder he travels, disappears for a week at a time. I force a smile, and he heads off down the hall. Now is my only chance. I slam on my shoes and flee out the front door. My heart jumps into my throat when an alarm begins to blare. Shit, I forgot about the security alarm.

I don't have my car, so I run like the hounds of hell are chasing me. When Mason first brought me here, I loved how isolated his home was. Now I know why. My footsteps echo down the darkened street and I try not to look back and slow myself down. I have no intention of being the dumb bimbo who trips and twists her ankle, allowing the psycho murderer to catch up.

If I can just get to the guard shack, somewhere where there are witnesses, I'll feel safer. I can call the cops, or Ian, or…I don't know. I can't think straight. My side is splitting and there's no sign of anyone coming after me, so I veer to the right, jumping a fence into the yard of an empty house with a for sale sign on the lawn. I just need to catch my breath. My hand is stinging and I vaguely notice blood dripping from my palm. I must've sliced it on the fence. My breathing slows a little as I lean against the house, shrouded in shadow. One minute, and I'll keep going.

How could he do this? I think of the past month we've spent together. His sweet smile when he watched me with the baby panda at the zoo, the way he played with Matty on his birthday, how he cared for me when I was hurt. I can't relate that man with the one who kidnaps women and sells them into sexual slavery.

I've seen some Alpha male behavior, of course. Tracking me down at the racetrack when I wouldn't call him back, having his security follow me without my knowledge when he thought I was in danger, beating the shit out of Danny when he attacked me. I know he's tough, and likes to be in control, especially in bed, which has been amazing, but I never saw the monster in him. Am I that blind, or is he that charming?

Why would he spend all this time making me fall in love with him? To what end? If he just wanted to fuck me, he had that. If he was out to kidnap me for his slave trade, he's had more than enough opportunity. Why take me to Turkey Run to make love under the stars or spend tonight taking goofy pictures at the carnival? I guess even psychopaths need company. Maybe he really does care about me, but it doesn't matter now. I could never be with such a horrible person, and he has to know I won't just go about my life letting him torture women while hiding behind a charity. He'll sell me or kill me. I have to get away.

My chest locks up as a hand falls over my mouth, and I'm dragged backwards through the yard. The taste of blood wets my tongue when I bite the hand pressed against my lips. "Fuck, calm down, I'm not going to hurt you." The voice doesn't belong to Mason. He must've sent someone after me. It's bullshit. If I can't escape, I'll either end up raped and chained in some third world dungeon or dead. I've seen the horror stories on television.

His arms lock around me, and no matter how hard I fight, I can't get loose. He shoves me into the driver's side of Mason's dark sedan and pushes me into the passenger seat. As soon as the car is moving, I dive out my door, rolling on the pavement before leaping to my feet to run.

"Goddamn it!" he yells, slamming the car into park and darting after me. I don't know why I bothered. I only get a few yards before I'm grabbed and thrown over his shoulder.

"Please, let me go. I'll never say anything. I just want to go home."

"Mr. Reed needs to speak with you." He puts me on my feet behind the car and reaches to unlock the trunk. Panic squeezes my ribs and I stomp on his foot as hard as I can, twisting to try to get loose before he can lock me inside. "Fine," he growls, and I feel the prick of a needle in my hip.

"No…no." My cries are fading along with my vision. A gray veil covers the world and I slump into the monster's arms as the darkness swallows me.

To be continued in Mason, Striking Back: Book Two.

Acknowledgments

Thanks to Jolanda Lovestoread for tweeting my books endlessly. She has wonderful book suggestions. Follow her here:

https://twitter.com/JolandaNovella

Special Thanks go to Lissa Jay and Jamie Lauritano for beta reading and saving me from embarrassing plot holes and ridiculous mistakes.

Last, but not least, thanks to all the book bloggers and page owners who make it possible for Indie authors to get their stories out there. We couldn't do it without you.

I love to connect with readers! Please stalk me at the following links:

https://facebook.com/authorsmshade
https://facebook.com/smshadebooks
https://twitter.com/authorSMShade
http://www.smshade.blogspot.com

Would you like to be a part of the S.M. Shade Book Club? As a member, you'll be entered in giveaways for gift cards, e-books, and Advanced Read Copies. Be a part of the private Facebook group and privy to excerpts and cover art of upcoming books before the public. You can request to join at:

https://facebook.com/groups/694215440670693

Thank you for reading! If you enjoyed this story, I hope you'll consider leaving a review on Amazon. It doesn't need to be long, a few sentences that share your opinion of the book would be very much appreciated.

More from S.M.

Mason, Striking Back: Book Two

From the moment I saw her, I wanted her in my bed.

I should've stopped there.

Everly Hall burst into my complicated life and changed it forever. I'm a fighter, but I had no defense against this beautiful, stubborn woman.

Now, I stand to lose everything I have, everything I am. My secrets are dangerous, and put more lives at stake than my own. I intended to tell her in time, but my time is up.

Everything rests on Everly.

This is the conclusion of Mason and Everly's story.

Contains violence and sexual situations and is intended for adults 18 and older.

Coming soon:
Parker, Striking Back: Book Three (10/2015)
Alex, Striking Back: Book Four (01/2016)

The Last Woman, All That Remains : Book One

When Abby Bailey meets former model and actor, Airen Holder, in a darkened department store, romance is the last thing on her mind. A plague has decimated the population, leaving Abby to raise her son alone in a world without electricity, clean water, or medical care. Her only priority is survival.

Traumatized by the horror of the past months, Abby and Airen become a source of comfort for one another. Damaged by her past and convinced Airen is out of her league, Abby is determined to keep their relationship platonic. However, Airen is a hard man to resist, especially after he risks his life to save hers.

When a man named Joseph falls unconscious in their yard, and Abby nurses him back to health, everything changes. How does love differ in this new post apocalyptic world? Can three unlikely survivors live long enough to find their place in it?

This is the first of the All that Remains series and can also be read as a stand alone novel. It contains violence and sexual situations and is recommended for ages 18 and older.

Falling Together, All That Remains : Book Two

In the aftermath of a global nightmare, Abby Holder is living her dream. Married to the love of her life, Airen, and surrounded by friends and family, it seems she's found her happily ever after.

But the struggle of living in a post-plague world is never ending. When circumstances take Airen far away, she's faced with the devastating realization he may be lost to her forever. Broken-hearted, she turns to Joseph, her best friend and the only one who understands her pain. After all, he loves Airen too.

The sound of a car horn in the middle of the night changes everything, leaving Abby caught between the two most important men in her life. After surviving the worst the world could throw at them, Airen, Abby, and Joseph must face the most brutal human experience...true love. Can they overcome the betrayal, the hurt feelings, and jealousy to do what's right for the ones they love?

Their circumstances are far from ordinary. Perhaps the answer is extraordinary as well.

This book includes sexual scenes between two men and is intended for ages 18 and older

Infinite Ties, All That Remains : Book Three

The more you look to the future, the more the past pursues you.

Abby, Airen, and Joseph have fought and suffered to come together. All they want is to move forward and raise their family with the love they never had.

Unfortunately, the re-appearance of former friends and enemies complicates their lives, threatening to expose closely guarded secrets. With a vital rescue looming, their relationship isn't the only thing at risk. Can they let go of the past in order to hang on to a future with each other?

This is the conclusion of the All That Remains Trilogy.

Sneak Peek at Landon, In Safe Hands: Book One

Check out the first chapter in Landon, the first book in the In Safe Hands Series.

Zoe

The bus is late, but with the stellar day I'm having, I'm not surprised. By the time I meet Frannie at our favorite downtown café I'm sweating like a whore in church. It must be nearly one hundred degrees outside, and if it were any more humid, I'd be drinking the air instead of breathing it.

"Sorry, Fran, bus was moving at the speed of sloth. Have you been waiting long?"

"Zoe Page, you need to get your car fixed," Frannie replies, pushing a lock of red hair behind her ear. Frannie has been my best friend since we met four years ago. It was my first day of work at a crappy fast food restaurant, and Frannie was my trainer.

Her first words to me were, "Welcome to hell. Flip those burgers."

"Actually, I need a job," I sigh, unfolding today's newspaper.

"Oh, girl, what happened? That asshole still harassing you?"

"He won't be harassing anyone for a while. I'm pretty sure his balls ended up lodged in his throat, courtesy of my foot."

Fran chokes on her drink. "You kicked him?"

"He shoved me into a room and tried to stick his hand down my pants."

"Did you tell your boss?"

"My boss is his mother," I reply dryly.

"Damn. So, you can't go back."

"My days of cleaning at the Stay-a Nite Hotel are over. I'll just have to deal with the disappointment." My eyes scan the help wanted page of the paper. "I need a new job fast. I've just saved enough to fix my car, but I need a steady paycheck first."

Frannie grins at me. "Let's go out tonight. My treat. We'll hit the club, drink and dance until we don't give a shit about anything."

"I don't know. I really need to figure out what I'm going to do."

"It's Saturday. You can't job hunt until Monday. You need to have some fun." Frannie blinks her bright blue eyes at me. She's gorgeous and men always drool all over her. In addition to beautiful red hair and stunning eyes, she's got a figure that would make a Victoria's Secret model jealous. Not that I'm jealous…much. I'm no great beauty, but I don't exactly scare children on the street.

"All right, but just a couple of drinks."

"Whatever you say, girl. I'm getting trashed and finding me a man to climb." Our waitress laughs as she places our usual order in front of us and retreats.

"Hey, look at this. What do you think?" I point to an ad in the paper. Housekeeper needed. Must be willing to work evenings and nights. Serious inquiries only. A phone number and address are listed below.

"Nights?" Frannie asks, looking dubious.

"Maybe it's cleaning offices after hours or something. I can't be picky. Besides, nights work for me. My classes end at two." I dig a pen out of my purse and circle the ad with a sigh. I can't believe I'm job hunting again.

* * * *

"Ethan!" I call, trying to get through the front door of our apartment while balancing three grocery bags.

"Damn, Zo, you should've let me go with you," my brother Ethan scolds, taking two of the bags.

"I just decided on the way home we need nachos for dinner."

Ethan grins at me and starts putting away the groceries. He's such a good kid and sure doesn't deserve the shitty hand he's been dealt. He moved in with me a little over a year ago when our parents kicked him out.

At only fifteen years old, I couldn't let him go into foster care. I told him we'd work it out, find a way to make it. Thanks to the help of a local charity for homeless gay youth, we were able to put a deposit on this two-bedroom apartment without blowing all my student loan money. I only allow him to work in the summer when it won't affect his schoolwork. He's set to become valedictorian if he keeps on the way he's going.

"What are you doing tonight?" I ask.

"Is it okay if Rob and Zach hang out? The new DLC is out

for Call of Duty."

"No idea what that means, but sure." Rob and Zach are his two best friends. "I'm going out with Frannie, so try not to burn the house down."

Most people would be hesitant to leave a bunch of sixteen year old boys on their own, but as a self-professed group of geeks, these boys are as trustworthy as they come. They'll spend the night playing video games, guzzling Mountain Dew and watching those horrible Japanese cartoons.

His friends show up right after dinner as I'm preparing for a night at the club. I rarely go out like this, bars and clubs just aren't my scene. I study my closet with a frown and finally decide on tight jeans and a clingy red blouse. I have no desire to spend the evening stuffed into a dress and uncomfortable heels.

"Jeans," Frannie moans, barging into my room.

"Save it. I want to be comfortable, not attract assholes."

"Babe, you'll do that no matter what you wear. Come on, the cab's waiting."

"Just a couple of drinks," I remind her.

"Yeah, yeah."

Fran squeals with excitement when the cab drops us at Chaos, one of the most popular Indianapolis nightclubs. Fran's painted on mini skirt and low cut blouse get us past the line and into the club. "What do you want to drink?" Fran shouts over the music and chatter.

"Kamikaze."

"That's what I'm talking about, girl!" She's right. I've had a terrible day and I just want to forget about it.

We grab a table upstairs, overlooking the dance floor, where the music isn't as loud, and dive into our drinks. "I'm going to fuck...him," Fran says, pointing out a tall, dark headed pretty boy.

"Pace yourself," I laugh. "There are plenty to choose from."

"So choose one."

"You know I don't do one night stands."

"You don't do anyone."

Sighing, I down my drink and move on to the next. "I have enough to worry about without any bullshit man drama."

"I love this song!" Frannie squeals, grabbing my hand. "Let's dance."

Once I'm on the crowded dance floor, the drinks and music lighten my mood. Eyes closed, I let the music flow through me and join the throng of writhing, sweaty bodies. I can shake my ass with the best of them and there's no shortage of men to dance with. Frannie laughs and flashes me a brilliant smile when she spots me dancing between two men.

The guy facing me is a cutie. Blond hair, blue eyes and a muscular body. He rests his hands on my hips, grinning at me when the song ends and says, "Thanks for the dance, beautiful."

"You're welcome." I swat at the guy who seems to think dancing behind me gives him the right to put his hand on my ass.

Blond Guy pulls me away and glares at him until he takes off, grumbling. "Can I buy you a drink?"

"I shouldn't. I'm seeing someone," I lie. "But thanks."

"Anytime, sweetheart." He heads off to sweet talk his next prospect while I head to the bar for another drink.

I'm really happy Frannie convinced me to come out tonight. It's the most fun I've had in months. I'm only twenty-three, but some days I feel forty. With so many responsibilities, I just don't have the luxury of partying and dating like a normal young woman. There's a kid depending on me to feed him and keep a roof over his head.

The young bartender nods at me as I order another Kamikaze and an ice water, hoping to fend off a morning hangover.

"Put it on my tab." A shiver runs through me at the deep voice coming from behind me, and I turn to gaze into the most amazing eyes. I stare for a moment, trying to decide whether they're blue or green before I remember what he said.

"Thank you, but I'll get it," I tell him, causing the corner of his mouth to tuck in with disapproval.

"I want to buy you a drink." His stubborn entitled attitude

annoys me.

"And I want to be ten pounds lighter and a million dollars richer. I don't get what I want, neither do you." I'm being a bitch, but I'm not in the mood to deal with another pushy male who can't take no for an answer.

After handing my money to the bartender, I make my way back to our table where Frannie is cuddled up with a dark headed stranger. She always goes for the tall, dark and handsome type. "Zoe, this is Jeremy. We met last week when he delivered a package to me." The package she's hoping to receive tonight is clear on her face, and I have to laugh at how outrageous she can be. It's why I love her. We're complete opposites.

"Nice to meet you," I reply.

"He's here with a friend. You should meet him." Here we go again. Frannie is determined to find me a boyfriend.

"Here he comes," Jeremy says, waving to someone behind my back. "Landon, this is Frannie and her friend…uh." He struggles to remember my name.

"Zoe," I say reluctantly, reaching to shake his hand as he takes a seat beside me. Well, hell. It's the ocean eyed guy who tried to buy me a drink.

"Zoe." I've never been crazy about my name, but coming from his lips it sounds sexy. "That's a beautiful name."

"Thank you. I got it for my birthday."

A dimple appears in his cheek when he smiles. He really is attractive, with dark hair that curls over his ears and thick shapely lips any woman would love to kiss. "Can I buy you that drink now?"

I shake my glass at him. "Still working on this one, thanks. Then I should be going."

"Dance with me."

"Is that an order?" I snort. This guy really needs to work on his social skills.

Frannie pulls Jeremy to his feet and grins at me. "Come on, Zo. One dance before you go. It's still early."

Landon smirks, and I want to kick him, but I agree to one

dance, and we all head back to the dance floor. The man can move, I'll say that for him. He grins at me and places his hands on my hips, guiding me to the beat. "So, do you hate men in general, or did I do something to offend you?"

"I'm just not interested in dating right now."

Damn, though, the way he moves his body against mine makes me want to rethink that decision. The song switches to a slow sensual beat and he spins me around, pulling me back against his body. His chest and abdomen are rock hard, and I love the feel of them pressed to my back. They aren't the only thing that's hard. He's as turned on as I am. His scent fills my senses, fresh and clean like the forest after a storm, as his soft lips brush up my neck to my ear.

"Good, I'm not interested in dating either."

"Glad we're on the same page," I breathe, trying to remember why I don't want this man. His hand travels up my ribs while his other arm keeps me pinned to his chest. The second I turn my head to look at him, his lips land on mine. Smooth and full, they push every rational thought from my head, and his tongue wastes no time finding its way into my mouth, licking and tasting. He completely devastates me with just one kiss, and the smug grin on his lips when we break apart says he knows exactly how he affected me.

My heart thrums as his lips travel back to my ear to proclaim, "I'm interested in getting you back to my place and planting my face between those luscious tits before I bend you over my bed."

My breath flees my body and I freeze, sure I must've heard him wrong. "Excuse me?"

"You heard me, Ms. Difficult. I'll make it good. Fuck you like you need. You'll love it. I promise."

Taking a step away, I turn to gape at him. "Does that actually work for you? Telling women you just met you want to fuck them?"

A smirk twists his lips, and I want to smack the smug look off his face. "Pretty much."

My phone buzzes in my pocket with an unfamiliar

number, and I look up to see Frannie waving Jeremy's phone. Nodding, I wave to her and she grins, shaking her ass. We developed this little system since Frannie is no stranger to one night stands. If she leaves with someone we don't know, she calls my phone from his, so I'll have his number. If she ends up chained in a basement, the cops will know where to look.

I glare up at Landon. "My friend is leaving and so am I. Good luck finding a woman willing to overlook your crude mouth and lack of social skills."

"Babe, my mouth can be crude in all the right places."

"Charming," I murmur, shaking my head as I push through the crowd and into the cool night. It only takes a moment to get a taxi and I settle back against the seat, closing my eyes. God, what a jerk. A rude conceited asshole. Who talks like that to a woman they just met? Bend me over the bed and fuck me like I need.

His words are still echoing through my head when I curl up in bed, though they have a different effect on me in the dark. That body. Those lips. I doze off and dream of the crude things his mouth could do.

Sneak Peek at All That Remains

I'm hallucinating. I must be. The stress has finally shoved me over the edge. I'm not seeing this. He can't be real. I close my eyes and count to three. It doesn't help.

A man really is standing in front of me. His shock and incredulity mirror my own. Mine, however, is multiplied by the fact that I recognize him. He's famous. Well, he was before everything went to hell.

I take a deep breath and find my voice. "Uh…um…hi."

He blinks and continues to stare at me. I understand the disbelief he feels, but it's disconcerting.

"Mom?" My son steps up behind me, his hand clamping onto my arm hard enough to leave bruises. "Who is this?" he whispers. Before I can answer, the man begins to yell.

"Jayla! Where are you?" he shouts, backing away from us.

A young girl rounds the corner and grabs his hand, her eyes widening as she sees us all standing there, frozen. "Airen?" she whispers.

"It's okay." He squeezes her hand, still staring at me.

Despite the strange and alarming situation, I'm stunned by his beauty.

"I'm sorry. You just surprised me. You're the first people we've seen in a long time," he explains.

"Me too...I mean...same here," I stumble. Great, the first person I've seen in three months, and I'm doing my Rain Man impression. I take another deep breath and try again. "My name is Abby, and this is my son, Carson."

"I'm Airen, and this is Jayla. Is anyone else here?" His eyes dart from side to side.

"No, it's been just the two of us since, well..."

"The plague," Jayla says.

"We're just looking for some supplies," Airen explains.

"Well, you came to a good place. Most of the town was evacuated early, so the stores are still well stocked." If you can stand the smell, that is. The grocery side of the store is the worst, but the smell of rotten meat and vegetables still permeates the entire place. "Where are you from?"

"I'm from New Orleans, and Jayla is from Atlanta. We've been traveling for a few months, looking for a good place to stay for the winter. Where are you from?"

"Originally, we're from Indianapolis, but we moved here about five years ago. This is a good place to live. We're close to the lakes, and the winters aren't too harsh. It rarely snows."

"Have you seen any other people?" Jayla asks.

"No, have you?" Carson questions.

Jayla shakes her head.

"Well, we have a cooler full of sandwiches and drinks in the truck." I hesitate, suddenly shy about my next question. "If you haven't eaten, would you like to join us for lunch? There's a picnic table next to the side entrance." I glance up at them uncertainly. "I'm sure you have as many questions as we do."

He smiles, and though my eyesight is hindered by the gloom of the blacked out department store, the sight still takes my breath away.

"Sounds good. We'll meet you outside."

While Carson and I unload the truck and set the table, my mind is spinning. People! Actual real live walking, talking people!

"Mom, wasn't that guy on television? I could swear that's him. Wasn't he on one of your crime shows?" Carson asks.

Frankly, I'm surprised Carson recognized him. Airen starred in the show Undercovers—not exactly a crime show—where he played the part of a male prostitute.

"I don't know, honey. If it is him, he may not want to talk about it, so please don't question him. Let him volunteer the information."

"Sure. Do you think they'll stay in town? I hope they do. They seem nice."

I sigh. He's as desperate for company as I am. Carson has been through so much, and I'm extremely proud of how he's coping, but he needs a friend. What twelve-year-old boy wants to be stuck with his mother twenty-four seven?

"We'll just have to see how it goes. Don't get your hopes up."

"I thought we might be the last two people in the world."

"Never think it." I hug him. "We survived, and now we know two others have also. There will be more people. We just have to find each other."

Airen and Jayla arrive with carts loaded down with clothing, water, and food. As we sit down to eat, the questions fly back and forth. We're so thrilled to talk to someone that we keep interrupting each other.

I'm so happy for Carson. He really needed a child his own age for company. Jayla is twelve years old, thin and petite with dark skin and hair. Her deep brown eyes shine with intelligence. Carson is smitten instantly.

While I'm half-listening to the kids' conversation, I'm trying not to outright ogle Airen Holder. It was fortunate we first met in the dark. If I had seen him properly, I'd still be trying to talk. He is beyond gorgeous. Television didn't do him justice. His black as night hair is thick and wild, matching onyx eyes that seem to shine from within. He's quiet, brooding even, but when he smiles it's enough to stop my heart. He has a perfect jaw line, high cheekbones, and a flawless complexion. The shorts and tank top he's wearing show off a Greek God's physique.

"So." Airen turns those mesmerizing eyes to meet mine. "What did you do, you know, before?" he asks.

"I was a librarian."

"You must like to read."

"Yeah," I mumble, showing what months of limited human interaction has done to my stellar social skills. I know I should return the question, but I really don't want to play dumb. I know how he made a living before.

Before. Such a small word that now contains lifetimes. Everything we did, everything we were, summed up in two syllables.

"You were an actor, weren't you?" I ask.

"Guilty," he replies with a smirk. "I didn't think you recognized me."

"I may have watched a few episodes of Undercovers."

"Or DVR'ed the whole season." Carson giggles, and Jayla smiles at him with her hand over her mouth.

"Guilty." I shrug. I know I'm blushing as I silently plan Carson's violent death. "Don't worry. I won't pester you for an autograph. I'm not the star struck type."

Technically, this is true. I'm not impressed by his fame. It's those eyes and smile that have me so captivated. I'm trying not to say something stupid and make a fool of myself. I don't want him to know how much his presence affects me.

"That's a shame. I miss signing autographs. I used to model as well. Does that change your mind?" An arrogant little grin flashes across his face.

I have to laugh. I'm having lunch with a famous model and actor. It's so surreal. "Would you like us to show you around town?"

"That would be great."

Abraham

God's will has saved me. I've been touched. He has truly blessed me with forgiveness. Two years in this filthy, unholy place. Two years surrounded by the scum of society. The pastor was right. He said if I gave myself to Jesus, I'd be saved.

They all died. When I hid in the kitchen pantry, they never even looked for me. Oh, I could hear the cries for help. The scum cried out for water, for a doctor, even for their mamas. As if I'd come. If God had wanted them to survive, he would have provided for them as he did for me.

First, I found two bottles of water that had rolled under the pantry shelf. Next, there were the crackers from the dead receptionist's purse. Finally, a tear in the fence of the prison yard allowed me to escape. He granted me freedom and his forgiveness so I can spread his word to the poor souls he left behind.

They will hear.

Chapter One

"Carson, bring in the eggs, please. After breakfast you need to fill the water tank."

"Okay. What are we doing today, Mom?"

"I'm going to do a few loads of laundry."

If you think washing clothes without a washer or hot water is an easy task, I urge you to try it. No matter how creative I've tried to be, the old fashioned washboard-slash-clothesline method seems to win. "I think Airen wants to take the two of you fishing."

Jayla makes a face. "I'll stay and help you do the wash. I'd rather wash dirty underwear than sit in a boat all day with those two. They think they're so funny."

"I heard that." Airen grabs Jayla around the neck and plants a kiss on her head. "You know you look forward to my jokes."

"Even though mine are so much better," Carson brags.

Jayla shakes her head in exasperation. "You're both equally terrible."

Listening to them go back and forth makes me smile. We have become comfortable with one another. I don't know if the extended period of solitude or the mental trauma we've all suffered caused us to bond so quickly.

Fortunately, Carson and I had chosen a house with extra bedrooms. I'd picked it for its two fireplaces and its proximity to Kentucky Lake.

We have acres of woods on one side of us with paths leading down to the lake. The rest of the house is surrounded by open fields Airen and Carson have dubbed "the yard". Since they're the ones who cut all the grass with riding mowers, I suppose they can call it whatever they like. The view is beautiful in every direction. I love to watch the sun rise over the lake, the water reflecting the soft colors of the sky.

Carson and I were thrilled when Airen and Jayla accepted our invitation to live with us. We had all been on our own for so long. The conversation I had with Airen in private was uncomfortable and embarrassing, but I knew it was necessary. He's so gorgeous, and I didn't want him to think I had ulterior motives. However, recalling it still makes me cringe.

"Look, Airen, I want you and Jayla to stay. I think things will be better and easier on all of us if we stick together. I just want to assure you, I'd never take advantage of the situation," I explained.

He gives me a confused grin. "Take advantage? How?"

The bastard. He knows what I'm getting at, but he's going to make me say it. "I'm not hitting on you or trying to be with you or um...anything." My face becomes redder by the second. "I don't want you to worry. I want you to know I wouldn't...do that," I babble.

His smile broadens, spreading across his face. Why does he have to be so hot?

"Do I need to swear to the same?" he asks in an innocent tone.

I suddenly have the urge to kick him. "I think we can both agree that's not necessary," I answer dryly, rolling my eyes. I head back indoors, but not before I see the look on his face. It's a mixture of surprise and another emotion I can't seem to place. Pity, perhaps.

He could've saved the acting skills for someone more gullible. I'm not exactly attractive. Oh hell, why sugar coat it? I'm ugly. I've been ugly since I was a child and long ago accepted it as a fact of my life. However, I've learned some things are better left unsaid. In the past, when I'd told people I was aware of my unfortunate appearance, they tended to think I was fishing for compliments or trying to get them to disagree. We have all known that annoying pretty girl who will announce she's ugly so others will argue it and call her beautiful. That's the absolute last thing I wanted. I just wanted to address the big ugly elephant in the room and get it out of the way.

All that aside, they stayed. Surprisingly, life has become routine if not exactly normal. After months of Carson and me living on our own even the childish bickering is music to my ears.

"Do I have to go fishing?" Jayla asks.

"I didn't intend to hogtie you and drag you through the woods. It's so beautiful today; I was hoping we'd all spend a little time on the lake. What do you say, Abby? I'll even bait your hook for you," Airen offers, flashing his million-dollar smile.

Three pairs of eyes stare at me awaiting an answer.

"I'll go if Abby goes," Jayla says.

"Fine," I agree, "but I'm not cleaning the fish this time."

* * * *

Airen pulls a lightweight, flat bottomed boat down to the edge of the lake.

"Is this the one you've been using?" asks Jayla.

"Mmm hmm." Airen nods absently.

"Why don't you take one with a motor so you don't have to row?"

"With these guns?" He flexes his biceps, drawing a snort from Jayla. "Who needs a motor?"

Airen tosses us each a life jacket and makes sure the straps are tight. We manage to get in the boat and launch it without tipping it over. The first few minutes are hectic and noisy as we get the hooks baited and cast into the water. I'm always paranoid someone will get a hook through their eye. I'm sure we have scared away every fish in the vicinity. We finally get settled and quiet down. The kids each have their iPod's so it's pretty peaceful.

I'm not watching my bobber as I should. I'm in awe of the beauty surrounding me. The leaves have changed, and the distant shore is a mass of color. Bright red-gold and orange fades to more muted shades of yellow with a scattering of brown and dark green patches. The grass along the shore is a brighter green in startling contrast to the dark brown of the soil and sand sloping gently to meet the water where clumps of cattails sway rhythmically.

I close my eyes and let my other senses take over. The breeze caresses me, tickling the little hairs on the back of my neck, and the sun feels warm on my face and shoulders. The combination is very pleasant. The lake and the forest are alive with sound. Waves lap gently against the boat. Dragonflies hum a few feet above us, backed by the rhythm of a woodpecker, hammering away. It's lovely, harmonious, and somehow melancholy.

Breathing deep, I try to absorb the beauty and tranquility in which I'm immersed. I feel something inside me loosen, and my body relaxes. When I open my eyes, Airen is gazing at me with obvious pleasure.

"Better?" he asks in a low voice.

"I see why you like to spend time out here."

He nods pensively. "Sometimes you just need to let it go."

"Let what go?"

"Everything," he says simply. "Abby, if you ever need to talk..." His voice trails off.

I force a smile. "Thanks. Really. I'm just not the talk about my feelings type."

He grins at me with a small shake of his head. "I've noticed."

"Back at you."

"Touché, but remember the offer stands."

"I'll remember. I do have one serious question to ask you."

"Boxer briefs," he replies, flashing a charming grin that releases butterflies in my stomach.

"Ha! I do your laundry, doofus. There's no mystery there. I've been wondering, why don't you have a southern accent if you grew up in Louisiana?"

"I took acting classes at Carnegie Mellon University's School of Drama in New York, and they taught me to break my accent." His lips curve with a roguish smile. "It was probably for the best, I mean, it's an unfair advantage to be this good looking and also have a sexy accent."

"You're possibly the most arrogant person I've ever met," I reply with a chuckle, peeking up at him.

"Only possibly?"

"Shut up. You have a bite," I point out as his bobber dips below the surface.

A few hours later, Airen and Carson are cleaning the fish while Jayla and I watch.

"I caught the biggest one," Carson boasts. Airen just smiles, but Jayla is having none of that.

"You did not. Airen's catfish is twice the size."

Carson cocks his head and looks at Airen, his cheeks red from the sun. "I don't know what we're going to do without an eye doctor."

"What are you talking about now?" asks Jayla, her hands planted on her hips.

"I'm concerned about getting you the glasses you obviously need."

"All right. It doesn't matter whose is bigger," I lecture. Airen grins and raises his eyebrows at me. "Don't you start," I warn, smothering a grin. "You'd better remember who's going to cook those fish."

Carson interrupts. "You mean these big, meaty fish the men caught?"

Jayla looks around. "I only see one man."

"Again, because you need glasses. You're just mad that you didn't catch anything."

"I did! You know it was too small, and we had to throw it back."

"I'm just surprised you could see it," Carson remarks smugly.

"Hey! Thing One and Thing Two, that's enough." They will go on all day if I don't intervene.

Jayla sticks out her tongue at Carson and turns her back to him, but ignoring him doesn't last for long. Walking back, Carson and Jayla are a few yards ahead of us on the trail.

"They argue like brother and sister, but look at them," Airen remarks, watching them fondly.

Laughing and talking together, Carson pauses for Jayla to pick a few wild flowers growing along the side of the trail. Typical kids. That's what we see. Happy, carefree kids.

"He's so much happier since you two came along. I was so worried and preoccupied trying to keep us alive, fed, and safe, I didn't realize how lonely he was."

"What about you?" He glances at me.

You would think after seeing him every day I'd be accustomed to his beauty. If anything, it has become more difficult to ignore. His dark eyes sparkle as the shafts of sunlight filtering through the trees strike him, giving his face a quality I can't quite articulate. My heart speeds up in response.

He has become more muscular, probably from hauling water, gas, and wood as we prepare for winter. When he removes his shirt and tucks it into his waistband, sweat glistens on his chest. It's distracting.

"What about me?" I reply.

"Are you happier?"

I hate it when he's so direct. "I'm good. You?"

"I'm hungry." He smiles, also dodging the question.

"I'll make lunch if you'll fill the generators."

"Deal."

Three gasoline generators sit in a row behind our house, a tangle of extension cords jutting from their sides and threaded through the dryer vent. The generators are loud, and having power cords weaving through the house, tripping us up is a pain, but it's our only option. Battery powered lanterns replace our lamps, freeing the limited outlets for the most necessary appliances, like a refrigerator and stove. We travel to surrounding gas stations to siphon from their tanks. I'm concerned about what we'll do if we run out. Fortunately, with an abundance of gas stations and vehicles full of fuel at our disposal, it will be a long time before that becomes an issue.

The truth is I worry constantly. The lack of electricity and running water are only the tip of the iceberg. There are no doctors, no new medicine being manufactured, and no way to get help in an emergency. If one of us would break a leg, how would we set it? What if one of the kids gets appendicitis? An appendectomy was nothing before—there's that word again—but now it's a death sentence. I try not to dwell on these fears, but they're always on my mind. We're alone. Horribly, desperately alone. I don't know how I ever sleep.

Then, there is the food situation. Currently, it's not a problem. The stores are full of canned and packaged food with no shortage of canned fruits, vegetables, and meats. Unfortunately, that is only a temporary solution since all of it is dated to expire within two years. We have a two-year window to become completely self-sufficient. This is where the librarian in me wakes up and stands at attention.

It's all about education. We have to learn how to grow and preserve our own food and treat our own illnesses and injuries. It's Little House on the Damn Prairie around here, no internet, no answers at our fingertips. Only books. I've spent almost as much time amassing books as I have collecting food.

After pillaging the library for books on gardening and water purification, I thought of the hospital. It's the last place in the world I want to go. It's the only place I know for sure there will be bodies. When I approach Airen about it, he's less than enthusiastic.

"You can get all of that stuff at the pharmacy," he argues.

"I found basic first aid supplies and medicine at the pharmacy. We may need some instruments from the hospital, and we definitely need the medical guides."

"Do you plan on performing surgery?" he asks with a smirk.

"You never know what we might need. One of the kids might need stitches or…something," I finish lamely. He looks at me with an expression of amused skepticism. Hmm, maybe it's time to straighten something out. "I'm not asking your permission, you know. I'm going."

"So damn stubborn," he mutters under his breath.

"Excuse me?"

"I said you are stubborn. If you insist on this ridiculous trip then I'm going with you."

"You don't…"

"I'm not asking your permission. We'll go in the morning," he snaps.

Airen doesn't speak to me for the remainder of the evening, but he's prepared for our excursion into the hospital the next morning. He's more than prepared with two high-powered flashlights and a set of walkie-talkies.

"They have a two-mile radius. The kids can stay in a nearby house and remain in touch with us," he explains. "We have one stop to make along the way."

Once in town, he stops to search through a police station and returns with two gas masks. That never occurred to me, although I did skip breakfast out of fear I'd be sorry later.

With the kids safely ensconced in a nearby trailer, we prepare to enter.

"Put your mask on, Abby. We stay together. Understand?"

I nod. He's so bossy, but I know he's frightened. We don the masks and enter the lobby. It's dark and empty with a horrid putrid smell, somehow sweet and rotten simultaneously. I hate to think of how strong it would be without the mask.

"You okay?" Airen's muffled voice is barely audible. I nod

and point to a sign, SURGERY, and we head in that direction. The Bluegrass Medical Center isn't exactly a hospital, although that's how everyone in this small town once referred to it.

It's a small, one level building with an emergency care wing on one side and patient rooms on the other. Two operating rooms are in the rear along with a recovery room, ICU, and a radiology department. To the right of the entrance is a small cafeteria, a staff break room, and a multipurpose room used for educational purposes.

I shift the empty backpack higher onto my shoulders as we push through the double doors separating the lobby from the hallway. Oh fuck. Oh, we shouldn't have come. This is too much. I freeze and squeeze my eyes shut. Airen takes my hand while I try not to breathe too deep. The stench is much worse. Of course, it is. The emergency room to our left is packed with corpses.

The remains of men, women, and children are scattered about the floor and lying on the benches and chairs. Gurneys line the hallway end to end, filled with plague victims, decomposing in the cool dark building. A shudder runs through Airen, and I instinctively move closer to him. After what seems like an eternity, but was surely only seconds, he points his light at the door at the opposite end of the hall. It's an operating room.

We make our way down the hall, careful not to step on anything. The OR is mercifully empty. In a small storeroom at the rear, I load up on surgical instruments. I have no idea what we need so I grab a little of everything.

Taking Airen's hand, I lead him out of the OR toward a row of offices and through a door etched Chief of Surgery. On a bottom shelf, we find thick medical reference books with diagrams and multicolored plates, most of which I couldn't understand if I had a hundred years to study. Luckily there are more useful manuals showing how to start an IV drip, calculate the dosage of antibiotics, and stitch and bandage a wound. We add them to our backpacks which are growing heavy.

We turn left out of the office into the back hallway where a corpse dressed in white sits behind a desk. It's impossible to tell whether it was male or female. I suppose it doesn't matter. We make a right down another hall leading to the cafeteria. This hall is clear although the patient rooms we pass are crowded with occupied beds. There doesn't appear to be anything useful for us to gather. My hand trembles as I point to the exit, and Airen speeds toward it, pulling me along. We burst into the sunshine and gloriously fresh air, flinging off the masks.

"I'm sorry," I sob, breathing hard. "Damn Airen! I'm sorry! I had no idea it would be that bad." Could I have really done that alone? I seriously doubt it.

"We made it," he pants. "I'm never going back in there and neither are you."

The things we got were worth it though.

* * * *

We begin to devote two hours in the late afternoon to learning all the survival skills we can manage. The kids have dubbed this time school, but Airen and I are hardly teachers. We study along with them. Carson and Airen seem to have a better grasp of the hunting skills, although all of us can shoot. We all focus on the gardening and water purification books since those are our number one priorities.

Jayla's interest lies in the medical manuals. We study the first aid books, and I insist everyone learns how to start a saline drip, give an antibiotic shot, and bandage wounds. We never know who will need help or who will be around to give it.

Airen is terrified of needles. I mean seriously phobic. He wouldn't even let Jayla prick his finger when she and I were playing with a blood sugar monitor. If I ever need a shot or an I.V., Jayla is definitely my first choice to administer it. She's so intelligent and nothing really seems to bother her.

Our days are pretty full. We spend much of our time with the chores of daily life with limited power and no running water. We study and learn new ways to take care of ourselves. Airen and I both worry about the kids missing out on their childhood. We don't want them to grow up too fast and miss out on their adolescent years. They should be spending them with friends, having fun and growing up.

However, some things are necessary. They have to work alongside us in the garden. We need all the help we can get. They haul wood, water, and gas, plus help with countless other chores. Still, we want them to have fun. We throw a football around, catch fireflies, swim in the lake, and toast marshmallows over a bonfire. Airen can sing and play the guitar which may be the sexiest damn thing I've ever seen. They love to sing and dance along with him.

We spent one hilarious morning together watching Carson and Airen try to jump rope. Jayla loves to skip rope, and she's a pro. It had been years since I'd attempted it, and I was pleasantly surprised to find I could still keep up. After laughing at Airen and Carson until our sides ached, we had pity on them and allowed them to spin the ropes for us instead. Jayla and I had a wonderful time. I guess you're never too old for Double Dutch.

On rainy days we hook up one of the video game systems or the DVD player, and watch movies or play games thanks to the generator. We also play cards and board games or just sit around the living room and talk. Jayla and Carson are talking more about their lives before the plague. It's as if they heal faster, and I envy their ability to laugh instead of cry over the memories. I don't seem to have the same skill, at least not yet. We've all become closer. It starts to feel like a family.

"Jayla's birthday is Saturday," Carson announces at dinner.

"I know." I smile at him. "What kind of cake would you like, Ms. Teenager?"

"Chocolate with chocolate icing and chocolate chips?"

"Would you like some chocolate with that?" Carson teases. "Some chocolate syrup or maybe we could crumble up a Hershey Bar?"

"I wouldn't turn it down." She laughs.

"Sounds good to me," I tell her. "Is there anything special you'd like to do?"

"We could hook up the Wii, and I can beat you all at bowling."

"Are all teenagers delusional?" Carson asks.

I'm trying to keep a straight face. "Hush, Carson. Jayla, that sounds like fun, and I'll make chicken stew for dinner." It's her favorite, with homemade noodles.

"I can't wait."

When Saturday comes, Jayla's thirteenth birthday is a success despite the dismal weather. It has been raining for nearly a week and everyone is starting to get a little stir crazy. The kids are moping around, sniping at each other, and I'm in a mood that I can't seem to pull myself out of.

Only Airen appears to be unaffected. Of course, he is normally quiet and broody so it would be hard to tell the difference. It's great fishing weather if you don't mind the rain and are as oblivious to the cold as he seems to be. He spends most of his days on the lake.

When night comes, I lie awake for hours, tossing and turning. Carson made a comment earlier this afternoon that won't quit haunting me. It's amazing I can be so tired, but as soon as I lie down, my brain decides it's time to solve all the world's problems. Which, if you haven't been paying attention, are pretty numerous.

Everyone has been asleep for hours when I throw on my sweat pants and move to the sofa on the porch. The wraparound porch is another part of this house I fell in love with. Screened in and furnished like a sitting room, it stretches along the front and left side of the house, with access to my bedroom and Airen's next to it.

I have an urge to see the stars, something I used to do whenever I was depressed, just sit and watch the night sky. It's beautiful. The stars are shining, and a few wispy clouds draw thin lines between them. How can this still exist when our whole world is dead? Billions of people are gone forever. Yet, the same cold stars, the same sliver of an uncaring moon stare down at an empty planet as though nothing has changed.

My chest tightens, and I keep trying to swallow the lump in my throat. I'm not a crier, and I especially hate to cry in front of another person, but tonight I feel so overwhelmed and hopeless I can't fight it any longer. When I recall Carson's innocent comment, "I'll never get my black belt." I lose the battle. The tears overflow as I despair of the endless list of things he'll never get to do.

I'm sitting with my knees pulled up to my chest, my arms draped across them, my head bowed and resting on my forearms, bawling like a baby when a hand gently rubs my back. Oh, how long has he been standing there? I know it's Airen. I can smell his orange scented soap, something I usually tease him about. I struggle desperately to stop crying. Breathing deep, I strive for control and a small sob escapes.

"Airen, please, I need a few minutes alone," I whisper, keeping my head down.

"No, you don't," he answers in a husky voice.

I obviously woke him. I'm torn, embarrassed that he caught me crying in the middle of the night. Still, part of me doesn't want him to leave.

He continues rubbing slowly up and down my back and asks, "What's wrong?"

I snort. What could possibly be wrong?

"I mean, is it something specific? Did something happen?"

"It's stupid." I can't tell him I'm crying my heart out because Carson will never get his black belt. It sounds ridiculous, but it encompasses so much. The life he should have had, all of the opportunities he's lost, that all of us have lost.

"Abby, I'm sure it's not stupid."

I just shake my head, keeping it down. The door squeaks as he goes back inside, and I sigh. I don't know if it's with regret or relief. I'm still struggling to get a hold of myself when he sits beside me. Without a word, he drapes a blanket across the both of us and slides his warm arm around me. It's all I can take. His concern and comfort push me over the edge, and I can't stop sobbing. He pulls me against his chest until I bury my face in his shirt and break down completely. I no longer care about being embarrassed. I'm past that. All the horror, worry, and grief overpower me. I'm drowning in it.

"It's okay," he murmurs. His chin rests on my head while

he strokes my hair. "You're okay. I've got you."

I finally get a tenuous grasp on my emotions and manage to calm down. Tears still run down my face, but at least I can breathe again. "I'm sorry," I mutter.

"You shouldn't be."

"I never cry."

"I know. I think that's your problem, sweetheart. You let it all build up," he says kindly. Even in my pitiful state, hearing him call me by that endearment pulls at something deep inside of me. "Will you tell me what's wrong?"

"Our kids have no future," I whisper.

He sighs. "They have a different future than we expected. So do we. None of us can predict what's going to happen, Abby."

"Did you know Carson studied Shotokan Karate for six years?"

"Yes, he mentioned it. I could learn a few moves from him." He pushes a strand of hair off my face and tucks it behind my ear.

"He was preparing to test for his black belt. His teacher told me he knew everything he needed to know. He was really good."

"He is really good," he interrupts. "I'm sure he still has the skills."

"But he'll never get his black belt, and he was so close. I know in the grand scheme of things it isn't important, but it was to him...and to me. I just wish I could have one more normal day. I want to watch my kid in his karate class and talk to the other parents. I want it back. I know it's ridiculous. I should be grateful we're alive, fed, and not alone." My tears are coming faster again.

"Shh, it's not ridiculous." He pulls me closer. "It's okay to grieve for the things you've lost and for the life you had before. It's normal. I feel the same way."

"You had a glamorous life, Airen. You lost so much more than I did. Yet, I'm the one crying and embarrassing myself," I mumble, shaking my head.

He sighs again and leans back to look at me. "My life wasn't glamorous or any more important than yours or the kids.

Look at me, Abby."

My cheeks flare, and I shake my head again. I can't look at him after crying all over him.

"Look at me," he orders in a stern voice. Tears shine in his eyes and trickle down his face. Oh, Airen. My heart breaks all over again. "You aren't alone. We're all grieving. We're all hurting. Please, don't be embarrassed."

I gulp and nod. "You should go to sleep. I'm okay, and I've already kept you up too late."

"Don't be silly. I'm not tired, and you're not okay." He emphasizes his words by wiping away the tears still running down my face. "But you will be. Come with me." His hand closes over mine, and I'm led inside to the living room. "I'm going to put a movie on for us. Any requests?"

"Whatever you want." While he goes outdoors to start the generator, I blow my nose and wipe my face even though I'm still crying. Damn! Get a grip, girl! I feel so heavy, like I'm sleepwalking, just going through the motions. I can't think. All I can do is cry. I've had enough humiliation for one night. I'm going to bed.

Airen will hear none of that talk. He carries a blanket and pillow to the sofa and orders me to lie down. I could almost laugh at his attitude if I could quit crying long enough. After he starts the movie, he surprises me by sitting on the end of the sofa and placing my head in his lap.

"I'm not going anywhere whether you like it or not," he asserts. "Try to sleep."

I can't help but giggle. "Yes, sir."

"Hush." He smiles and rubs my arm as he focuses his attention on the television. I give up. I have never been so tired in my life, so emotionally and physically drained. I turn onto my side and press my forehead against his firm stomach.

"I'm sorry. You know this isn't me, Airen. I'm stronger than this. I'll get it together." Things are tough enough without having a hysterical woman to deal with.

"Stop apologizing. You don't have to handle everything alone, Abigail. You don't give yourself enough credit. No other woman would have lasted two minutes in that hospital, and you were going to go in alone."

"I'm glad you were there," I murmur, relishing the sound of my name on his lips.

"Me too." The last thing I remember before falling asleep is feeling his fingers run gently through my hair.

I wake to the sound of Jayla and Carson laughing. They're eating cereal and challenging each other to a game of Rummy. The memories of the night before invade, and I bury my face in the pillow. How am I going to face Airen today? What did he tell the kids? I've never slept in the living room.

As if in answer to my unspoken question, Carson asks, "When can we stay up all night watching movies?"

I miss Airen's response as I realize this is his explanation for my sleeping on the sofa and probably his exhaustion.

After they head to Carson's room to play cards, I get up and dress. I still look like hell after brushing my hair and teeth, but it will have to do for now. Airen's knocking on my door. So much for avoiding him. I suppose it's better to get it over with.

He smiles at me. "Hey."

Oh, that smile. "Hi."

"I just wanted to see how you're doing."

"I'm good, and I'm sorry I—"

"Stop," he interrupts, holding up his hand. "There's nothing to be sorry for, Abby. Don't apologize."

I force myself to meet his eyes. Damn, they're so dark. Impulsively, I throw my arms around him and hug him hard, closing my eyes when his arms tighten around me.

"Fine, I won't apologize, but at least let me say thank you." I have to say it because I know how similar we are when it comes to hiding our emotions, and how hard it must have been for him to let me see him cry. Yet, he had, so I wouldn't be as embarrassed.

"You're welcome, darlin'." Oh.

His face is pink when I let him go and...oh hell. He's so breathtaking standing there in only sweat pants, bare chested, and bare footed. I have to stop staring at him.

"You know, your accent sneaks in sometimes."

"It's worse when I'm drunk," he replies with a laugh.

"I really do feel better. Can we just pretend I didn't have a meltdown last night?"

"Sounds like a plan."

Abraham

Is he one of the faithful, Lord, or is he one that needs to be brought into your light? He appears to be a normal man, but it's so difficult to separate the innocent from the heathens. I have watched the man named Cole for over a week, and I've observed no deviant behavior. When I searched his home I found a bible, although I can't be certain it belongs to him and not the house's former occupant.

I observe him through his bedroom window as he prepares for bed. He kneels at the end of his bed to pray.

"Thank you for getting me through another day, God, and for Katie. I was going crazy being alone all the time. I pray there are more of us out there. Humankind isn't going extinct, are we? Please, don't let that happen to us. Please, let us find more survivors. Please, watch over my wife and sons since I can longer do it. I hope they're really with you. Amen." He sighs and crawls into bed alone.

I think I can trust him. The woman, however, I'm not as confident about. They sleep in separate rooms, and I've witnessed no fornication. Yet, I haven't observed any signs that she speaks to God nor reads his word. Woman has always been the downfall of man. I intend to watch her closely.

I think it's time we all meet.

Troy

"Hey, buddy! What are you doing up there? You aren't going to jump are you?"

The man looks down at me as if I'm a figment of his imagination. He's sitting on the edge of a metal beam high above the bridge. I don't know what river I'm currently crossing, but the water is fast moving, and I doubt that he's contemplating a swim.

"Have a heart, man! I'm tired of my own company! All of this solitude is boring as hell! Come down the slow way and I'll buy you a beer and a new car!" I call up to him. I've been totally alone for almost six months, and it's enough to turn the most stable person into a raving lunatic. I'm not at all surprised this guy was ready to take the high dive. He looks confused and unsure of what to do next.

"You don't want to swim in that water, man! Unless you want to glow in the dark or grow a third nipple!"

He begins to work his way down. Whew! I'm dizzy just watching him. Heights are not my friend. He approaches me carefully. What do you say to someone who was probably seconds away from offing himself? "Hi, I'm Troy."

"Micah," he replies, shaking my hand as if nothing out of the ordinary just happened.

"Do you mind if we move off of this bridge? I'm not a fan of heights."

He laughs. "Sure."

We spend the next few hours talking. Well, questioning each other. After about four thousand questions get tossed back and forth we have a general idea of what the other person has experienced. It comes to the same end, of course. Everyone we cared about has died. Everyone we've ever known is dead. At least neither of us had children. Micah had a live-in girlfriend of two years. I lost a group of friends who had become my family. We've both been completely alone since the plague. Oh, and we both have nice hair.

Micah doesn't even blink when I tell him I'm gay. I have a few seconds of hope that he may be also before he responds.

"That's cool. I'm straight, though."

"I saved you for nothing," I say with a grin.

"Sorry to disappoint you," he replies sarcastically. We're sitting on a porch of a small house facing the river.

"Why did you pick this house?" I ask.

"It's close to the river."

"That it is. I'll bet when the wind blows just right you can smell all of the sewage in Illinois."

"Seemed like a smart idea to live near the water."

"Yeah, it probably is. So, you intend to live now, do you? Do I need to watch for you to wander off in the middle of the night? Maybe I should remove your belt and shoelaces?"

He snorts and shakes his head. "I'm not going anywhere."

"Good. That water was probably cold. I'm sure there are worse ways to go, though. Like diving head first into a wood chipper."

Micah laughs and runs his hand across his forehead. "I think feet first would be worse, actually."

"I suppose you're right. How about doing a cannon ball into the mouth of a volcano?"

"Or hanging yourself with a bungee cord. That would be time consuming."

"Seriously though, would you really have jumped?"

"Since I've climbed up there three times now, I doubt it. I wanted to. There just didn't seem like there was any point in being the last guy alive."

"Loneliness is a bitch," I agree. "I say we get drunk."

"Hell of an idea."

Printed in Great Britain
by Amazon